Taming of a Brew

SITA SEECHARRUN HARRIS

ISBN: 9798598196694

DEDICATION

I would like to thank my husband Ray, for his support, unfailing belief in my writing and patient ear to listen to my script.

My late Mother, Devika, who would have been proud to read this book today.

ACKNOWLEDGMENTS

As one of the most consumed beverages in the world, tea is virtually everywhere. But what exactly is tea? Is it a drink? A cure for cancer? A gateway into mysticism? A skin balm? Is it a flower? An herb? Or, is tea just another consumer-packaged product? Living away from my native island, it suffices to taste a cup of tea from Mauritius for me to be transported back to its lush cool highlands. Be it Vanilla laced, or of mere natural aroma, the Mauritian tea is proudly served in all the five-star hotels and on board the national airline to taste 'Mauritius' immediately. If you are a serious tea drinker, a casual tea drinker, or someone merely curious about one of the world's great crafted agricultural products, this book should provide something of value and interest as a prelude to a drama cum romance with the backdrop of a tea estate.

My hope in writing this book is that my native island of Mauritius, which is known for its beautiful beaches and stretches of sugar cane fields in lush hues of green. What is barely spoken about, is its tea cultivation, which carve a special place in the flora and post-colonial landscape of the island.

Throughout the book, I have tried to remain aware that tea's power and magic are not found in its leaves, in the liquid it creates, or in our relationship to these things, but in its ability to help us feel connected to our shared humanity. I had gleaned a great deal from my years in the corporate world. My job has taken me right across the planet. I knew how to get things done, and the kind of business I didn't want to be in. I didn't subscribe to cronyism, old boys' clubs or the tacit understanding that ethics come second to shared values. All I wanted was to get involved in something that actually meant something to people's lives.

My travels took me to paths I didn't know existed in terms of tea and that it thrives in such a monumental variety besides what I knew from my own island. From the misty hills of Darjeeling, Assam, to Ceylon (Sri Lanka), the foothills of Kilimanjaro in Tanzania, the Dao inhabited valleys in the mountainous regions of Sapa in Vietnam. I discovered, learnt and appreciated this brew in all its intricate and complex forms.

This has also led me to some of the best restaurants, past smooth tablecloths and cool dining rooms, into the heat and clamour of the kitchens, and to the most fascinating chefs in the world. Tea has introduced me to builders, artists, teachers, actors, athletes, perfumers, hoteliers, sommeliers, baristas, fishermen, pilots, diplomats, expats, homemakers, friends and complete strangers. I was time and again consumed by one common link I shared with each person, through a cup of tea.

A pause. A conversation. A confidence.

Renewal of a friendship or saying goodbye, tea was always the main actor on stage.

Waking up in a really good hotel and ordering breakfast in bed is a great luxury. There is no need to get out of the warm nest and make it yourself. To have tea brought to you, allows you to stay longer in that delicious drowsiness. The problem is, room-service tea isn't always very good. The worst is when a cup of hot water is brought with a teabag lying enveloped on the saucer. By the time the waiter has brought the tray up from the basement kitchen, through the service passageways, up in the lift, down the corridor to your room and then waited for you to open the door, the water is, at best, tepid. However hurriedly you dunk the bag, it lies there on the surface. You attempt to sink it with the teaspoon, but it bobs. Pale clouds seep from the bag and vaguely colour the cool water. It's all but impossible to get much flavour going – the concoction tastes mostly of paper bag.

Given that a tea's best flavours, as a rule, dissolve in the first ninety seconds, your tea will probably be very over-infused. You pour the first cup and its subtleties will likely have been subsumed by the tannins. Tannins are a type of flavonoid molecule in tea that contributes two characteristics: bitterness and astringency. The astringency-that dry feeling in your mouth- comes about because the tannins attach themselves to proteins in your saliva that would normally help lubricate. Tannins really do dry out your tongue. But they also bind to other proteins and fats, so the presence of milk in your tea or cream on a scone reduces the effect.

If you use milk to balance and dilute your tea from the over-stewed pot, it might be okay. The milk is cold, and the tea has been sitting cooling for a long while. When you add the milk, it makes your tea cold. If it's a green tea, it's utterly ruined before it reaches your room.

There is a solution, of course. The dry tea is

weighed into a pot in the kitchen and the water is poured into a thermos flask to keep it at the ideal temperature. The room-service waiter then brings it to the room and doesn't pour the first cup's worth of water onto the tea until he's put the tray down on the table. You can then infuse the tea to your desired strength. With the thermos of hot water, you can reinfuse the leaves repeatedly as you enjoy your breakfast.

My dreams of tea have been infusing, quietly, for some time. Until, I decided to pen it all out and make this book come true.

So, in my vast journeys, I cannot mention enough all those who taught me, shared their knowledge or passion about tea, nor the best friendships that were bestowed to me around a cup. I can say thank you for gifting me with memories that would forever linger, and taste, that my mind will always remember.

1 DEVIKA

Three days ago, when the bougainvillea bushes spurted their most colourful bracts, and the lychees bent the laden tree branches to the ground, Devika packed her belongings and left Plaine des Palmistes. In her bouncing belly was me, bathed in amniotic fluid, coiled up and in no hurry to come out into this world.

The sky had taken a murky reddish tone, and a strong breeze had picked up menacingly. The elders always said that a storm would break suddenly when the heavens showed the colour of red lentils, so Devika hastened her step keeping that in mind. A neatly folded envelope contained a letter of four pages in fine lightweight vellum, cursively written spilling news which was heart breaking. Devika had received it a week ago, and ever since she had not parted with it, reading it as many times as she could and still get startled by its content, in utter disbelief.

The long drive was in complete silence, Devika stared blankly at the sugar cane fields which stretched away in an extensive patchwork of greens and black basalt rock mounds like Aztec temples to appease the gods.

The flowers of the canes swept in all directions in a soft wave of purplish silvery inflorescence, heading the breeze. There wasn't much to see aside from the roads between the Servian and Boucher plantations, which were dusty with red terracotta soil and lined with fat garnet coloured sugarcane. Some of these reed-like plants were up to twenty feet tall and the streets looked like freshly cut swathes through the lush greenery. Rain was intermittent. At this time of the year, it was the most predictable daily happening. Always finding a gap to announce itself before the deluge would break, swelling rivers, canals and tributaries into milky tea like rapid flows.

A water puddle gave the vehicle a sudden hiccup and Devika woke up from her reverie. She had secured a small two-bedroom house in Port Louis and was on her way to her freedom. She had broken away from her in-laws after the damning letter she had received. Her husband had bid her adieu in the most elegant written narrative without any apology and had asked her to move on with her life without him. He had found someone else to warm his sides in the chilly London city he was living in now. He did not even bother to ask about the child ready to be born. Such was his indifference, which caused more than a heartbreak in Devika.

She was in a state of shock but felt unusually

strong. Probably, hormones were prepping her spirit for my arrival. At the new house, she unpacked her belongings, after the driver had unloaded some boxes and furniture. A simple meal of watercress and rice with a fried egg gave her a well-deserved break to the long and stressful day. Just because a child hides away the wound, and tries to learn to smile, it doesn't mean she's dealt with it. It just means she can act well.

She picked up a dry palm leaf, cut in a round shape with a handle from the glass-topped gallery table and began to fan herself vigorously. The sun's rays were shining in their golden cloak in all corners of the room and the air was getting warm and humid.

This day was not going to be an ordinary one. It was her day of complete freedom. Now, alone with her unborn baby, the air, wind, sky, earth and nature witnessing how pain can turn into passion. Living life against all odds. She could never stay negative for a long time. Soon, she started moving around the room unpacking the boxes, filling out the shelves and cleaning the place thoroughly. Later, she found deep slumber out of exhaustion. Her heartbeats quietened and the baby rocked to sleep too.

The next morning when she woke up, Devika's mind was foggy and her eyes stung as if she hadn't slept well, but the world was no longer spinning, and the sense of essential wrongness was receding. She shook her head lightly, as if to clear it. She wasn't meant to be here. She had been somewhere else. She had been inside; she was almost sure, or she had been watching people who were inside. Somewhere very clean and white and with a big curtain which swished on its track ... reminding her of the house she left.

2 BONNE ESPÉRANCE

She had a good nose. Not its shape, which was fairly ordinary, but it sat in perfectly well with her other features. However, her sense of smell was uncommonly acute. Admittedly, a good sense of smell is a definite advantage if all you had to create were perfumes. Devika was just a part time florist.

'Is there anything else you'd like me to do before I leave for the day, Mrs Booj, I mean Binda?' She looked up from the bouquet of pink anthuriums she was tying thinking how lucky she was to secure this job. A month ago, she felt lost and didn't have a clue how to start her life as a single mother with a new baby. Things were starting to fall into place, step by step. Her temporary job allowed her to feed herself and her baby and pay for the roof over their heads. She would need to find a better job soon, if she is to think more seriously about Beti's future. The baby is very quiet and sleeps abundantly. She seems to have come from the world of slumber, related to Hypnos himself.

A beaming innocent face welcomes Devika each time she goes to the crib when her baby wakes up. The latter is not a grumpy wake. God only knows what this little thing will become when she grows up. As for now, she seems to be blessed with the most content demeanour.

The post-box was full when Devika reached home. Out of the pile of mail, she pulled a grey envelope which had a familiar 'Ministry of' heading on it. Excitement and anticipation made her hands shake as she opened the letter. An approval for a job she had applied for, which should conclude her days as a florist.

Devika also noticed a white envelope in the pile of the mail, with neat handwriting in blue fountain pen ink which had smudged around the edges from some drops of water. Probably the postman was caught in the earlier flash shower. Nothing looked familiar in the address on the back of the envelope. Who could it be from? She had not shared her new residence address with anyone. She opened the letter cautiously hoping it might be from her husband at his new address, but it wasn't his handwriting. Its content surprised her.

Today seemed to be pouring good news. With her heart thumping and still in disbelief, she reached for the phone and called her close friend, Peddy, omitting to tell her the content of the second letter.

Peddy immediately invited her to join in for supper with her family to celebrate the new appointment. After some good Rosé wine was cheerfully drunk, good hearty jokes exchanged and delicious food eaten, Devika left with a strange tickle of happiness in her heart. Maybe the universe was aligning to make place for her and her daughter in the sunshine of the big world.

She re-read the letter she had received from Belgium. It was from her uncle's solicitor, informing her of her inheritance for his vast tea estate. There were approximately three hundred acres of land, traditionally the hunting lands but now with a tea the plantation established after the British left.

It had a name: *Bonne Espérance*, which meant Good Fortune.

A new secured job, an inheritance of a massive estate, the young woman didn't know what to think of. Her uncle made a fortune after landing in Mauritius following the indentured migration. He had two brothers who chose to go to South Africa, they kept in touch. After Devika's father died, she didn't have much correspondence from her uncle. Now, this letter sealed the long years which separated her from him. A tea estate! What does she know about tea? And how to run a tea estate? From a young age Devika was conscious of the great family adventure that had taken place in 1843, an undertaking without precedent in the history of relations between Mauritius and India. In that year, a party of no fewer than seven members of their family had embarked for the British colonies. Now, the time had come to revive the past and lead it to new horizons. She could not falter her steps which had no grounding. She will have to rely on her instincts, a good star and plenty of perseverance.

So, that night, she made her decision to take up the challenge and accept what fate had thrown to her. A tea estate to look after, develop and flourish. The following days, boxes got packed, furniture waxed and ready again to be moved.

To reach her new home, she had to travel a winding narrow road without any houses in view until there came a huge deserted looking mansion that invariably drew her eyes. A white colonial villa sat isolated and lonely, on a road that had more twists and turns than a maze, that leads a mouse to the cheese. A far cry from the urban two roomed house she had just left in in the city.

There was a eucalyptus forest on the right-hand side from where the Moka range could be seen in the distance, in a blue violet haze. A strange fog had gathered in wisps and not far away great billowing waves could be heard from the coast. The landscape felt romantic and mysterious too.

A cool breeze suddenly picked up and Devika walked up to a front veranda which ran across the whole width of the house. The nearby peaks were wreathed in afternoon mist. Devika let down her bags and looked around her, thinking that in the cooler climate of the highlands, she and her baby would be in far better form. She was mentally eager to prepare for their new life on the plantation.

On every surface, bright blue and terracotta pots brimming with geraniums rustled in the breeze while two rocking rattan chairs rocked on the front verandah. 'This is beautiful,' Devika said to herself, as she walked up the terracotta-tiled steps. The warm air and pretty scenery had already made her switch off. She felt as if a valve had been pulled out of her side, letting out a long stream of stress. As she looked around and held her face up to the sun, her whole body relaxed.

A big white door led to the vestibule and the whole place smelled of mould and ginger. Le Pouce and Pieter Both mountains stood tall and proud within deep folds in the earth's crust, a drapery of dense, vivid green covering a gigantic, recumbent body. Between the rugged flanks lay a bowl-shaped valley. It was there, in the embrace of the jungle, that stretches of the tea plantation undulated until the horizon. She had reached the place where the entire, as yet unlived reality of her life awaited her.

'I think I can do it,' she heard herself whispering.

While thinking and packing, after some quick research, her conclusions were that the climate would be too wet for a good coffee yield; the old government plantation would have had ran wild since her uncle's demise; the pathways were probably overgrown; the terrain was too uneven as far as she could recall, with steep slopes and impenetrable swathes of jungle; it was too isolated, so transportation of produce would present enormous difficulties. Besides, would there be sufficient labour to be found on the sparsely populated high plateaus? But it was at that first moment – the sweeping view! the green lustre of myriad treetops! Her heart was set the moment she saw it.

Bonne Espérance, a baby, and a challenge to run a vast tea estate, had she made the right choice? Only time could tell.

Devika heard a voice behind her, soft and whisper like, she turned around and a young woman was standing by the door, like an apparition. Her dewy skin was a milky coffee tone, cascading dark hair held in a loose bun and her dress was plain, white and tidy.

“Hello Madam, I am Veronique, the daughter of the keeper. I look after the house and the kitchen, should you require anything, please let me know. I welcome you to Bonne Espérance.”

“Oh hello, you may call me Devika, actually I didn’t know that there was someone living here, already. I thought the property was empty.”

“The house has never been emptying as such. I grew up here”

The two women exchanged some pleasantries and the baby was glad to meet someone else to hold her. Véronique was a great friend of the Mauritian flora. She put all of her pride into cultivating as many species of the island's orchids as possible in the garden, supporting Uncle Marcel, who was also the gardener. The pampered acacias, and thirty-foot-high Allamanda vines with their bright lemon-yellow flowers gave the plantation its little ray of sunshine. A giant Tamarind tree dominated the centre of the garden, offering shade under the intense sun. There were lamps hanging on its branches. "Isn't it beautiful?" Veronique said joyfully, pointing at the decorations.

"I decorated the garden yesterday with my brother. You see that red lamp up there? That's mine – I made it! It contrasts beautifully with the flame trees and the Allamanda flowers "

Devika noticed how the red waxed floor of the verandah shone and looked spotless, giving the potted indoor ferns, in their exuberant green, a freshness only tropical houses exude. She should have picked up that this place was indeed well looked after.

“Madam, would like some juice or tea? May I

show you to your room, and maybe the baby needs feeding? What is her name?"

"I would really like that, thank you. She is my Shakuntala, my Beti"

"How adorable, so Beti, do you want to come to Aunt Vero?" The baby who loved anyone who would pick her in their arms, was already showing squints of joy in her wide dark eyes. Devika remembered the strange remark by the nurse who helped deliver Beti,

"She has keen curious eyes to see the world, your daughter will be bright and travel the world" Devika at that time wasn't tuned in to her baby's eyes, just then as her sorrow was crashing around her. But today, a new life awaits her, and things have not been too bad, so far. Véronique, had disappeared with the baby, already keen to take care of her.

A simple, but nicely cooked meal of pumpkin with its greens was served to Devika, accompanied with salted fish *rougaille*, steamed rice and black lentils. Fresh papaya and pink guava were refreshing as desserts. Savouring a cup of vanilla tea afterwards, made her heave with happiness. Life was just contouring a blissful future for her, indeed.

If things didn't work out with tea, she could switch to coffee, of which she had garnered a fair amount of knowledge during her year’s apprenticeship at her grandmother's place. She was resigned to this: she knew the wheels of bureaucracy on the island turned slowly. In the meantime, she would go ahead, she would start preparing for planting the land where she had chosen to live and work. All presented a good climate, enough rain and constant mist, and importantly, fertile land. The topsoil, two to three feet deep, was soft and crumbly, clay mixed with volcanic grit. Next, she would need to assess the manual workforce ready to give the plantation it’s required effort to sprout quality tea.

Flashes of her childhood memories brought her

images of days when sugar and tea plantations were the backbone of the island's source of wealth for the white landowners. Much earlier when slaves were planting sugarcane, having been taken away from their African tribes, they were brought in large ships during their long voyage, under atrocious conditions. A whip and nonstop labour summed up the realities of their lives. While working, they hardly looked up, which the sirdars would note with satisfaction. After all, they shouldn't be wasting time and watching anything going on around them but working. He would nod approvingly at the overseer. With time the master's attitude and behaviour mellowed. But one thing he didn't like was the slaves singing! However, some overseers promised higher yields if the men swung the machetes to the rhythm of a song. Every now and again, singing could be heard coming from neighbouring sugar cane fields, next to Bonne Espérance. Uncle Mohan didn't care for it much and preferred the silence. He believed that this lush green landscape needed all the calm and serenity it deserved.

3 SETTLING IN

Cyclones are notorious for wreaking havoc on the island, and on people's lives. December is the month when they start to show their destructive tails, disguised under romantic names of a boy or girl next door: Carole, Gervaise, Alix, Denise, Claudette, Laure, Flore, Hollanda. Old folks said that the 'female' cyclones are the most fearsome ones. An alert of cyclone Class I intensity would be heard on the national radio, prompting everyone to be on their guard. The veracity of a full-blown cyclone would see the whole island shut down and people glued to their radio day and night, waiting to hear the drop from class four back to one again. Very often the strong winds come first before the rains. Everyone will rush to the nearest Chinese shop to grab as many candles, and canned foods as they can, some last vegetables from the market stalls before prices shoot to the roof. Another cyclone under a female name, showed its colours a month ago. A whole hillside of buildings appeared to have vanished; the native bazaar was reduced to a patchwork of makeshift stalls and huts cobbled together out of salvaged wood and tarpaulin. Devika never realised how frantic and difficult life could be, living in the countryside. In the city, a cyclone for her was a matter of electricity shortages for a week, some branches torn down and leaves littering the courtyard. Here, things are much on a grander scale than she could ever have imagined. Time went slowly for Devika and her baby as she discovered the house, and its surroundings. She also had to get acquainted with those who regularly visited the place. The mattress maker who came once each year to strip the old mattresses and beat up the cotton fill, stitching a plump one with brand new covers. The pest controller who came regularly to spray the house for mosquitoes and other insects. The roof maintainer, who climbed to inspect the wooden tiles, which tended to move with the frequent cyclones. Devika was finding the pace of life at the villa very peaceful. Life was just flowing, if only there were no other pressing issues to address. It would be one long slumber.

*

On a fine day, Devika visited the village nearby as she did every fortnight. She went to what looked like a newly repaired house with its shining galvanized zinc roof. It was a local tea house she had been to each time she was in the village. It was held by a widow and her daughter, who had grown fond of Devika. The latter brought her thoughtful gifts each time.

The red coloured earth had bled itself to all the

walls, like rising damp with a terracotta dirt hue. Canopies of chayote vines matted a green wall around the house, some hens cackling and pecking on the side. Lisette, hearing Devika call out her name, turned around. She nearly dropped her tray of dirty teacups in astonishment. The Mistress herself!

'Well, well, Miss Lisette,' Devika said with a look of appreciation, 'you've grown into a beauty.' Lisette laughed, her fair face turning pink at her admiring look. Lisette knew she must look sweaty and dishevelled. It was late afternoon on a hot Saturday. If she'd known the mistress was going to appear out of the blue, she would have worn a frock instead of slacks under the old-fashioned apron, put on some lipstick and brushed out her dark hair instead of tying it back with a rubber band.

"So, how is the tea house coming on? Busy?"

"It's not bad, many people stop by now, and more men than women. At least, it's good that they drink tea and coffee instead of getting drunk on rum at the Chinese shop. What can I get you Madame? We have *thekua*, and hot gâteaux piments. Mother is just bringing some *massepain* soon.'

"Please call me Devika, I would very much like some gâteaux piments, and a hot coffee please."

"I will get that for you ...Devika"

Lisette had squeezed into the flowery frock she was wearing. The short sleeves pinched her fleshier young bust.

'Your dress fits nicely, mind you I wish I had a figure like yours.'

'Thanks, Devika,'

'You're much more diplomatic than Mother; she calls me *'patate'* Says I eat too many of her delicious *faratas.*'

'Well, I wish I was your shape. After a baby,

you know, things are not ever the same again.'

Lisette laughed, incredulous, as Devika looked so beautiful. Beauty does not come to everyone. Some women wear it without being conscious while others flaunt it until it looks vulgar, thought the young girl. But the Mistress wears her beauty under what seems like a sad mask. Soft long hair adorns her bright face with wide brown eyes and a pert nose. She was petite in frame but exuded grace and confidence. Everyone at the plantation had heard of her taking over the place but most didn't know what she looked like nor what sort of person she was going to be with them.

Devika enjoyed her quiet moment with a delicious cup of home-grown ground coffee with milk, and some piping hot gâteaux piments. Lisette chatted a bit with her before rushing to attend to some customers. Devika left a cardigan for her at the counter before she left.

*

Veronique has been impatient all morning. The baby has been good and slept after her bottle feed. She was eager to ask Devika what to cook for lunch and dinner as the vegetables seemed a bit low in the pantry.

'You look just like your mother at your age,' said a voice behind her. Her Aunt Maude was visiting and wandered into the house.

'Too thin, you should eat a bit more of potatoes and Zack' Her frown deepened. She couldn't pronounce her j's. 'Jacque became Zack, and 'termoss' for 'thermos'. In this part of the island, the Mauritian accent resounded with more African tones. Like drops of rain on a tin corrugated roof, all sound merged into one in unison. Slaves and indentured labourers bore the same cross, that of serving the master, come rain or shine.

The soil is very fertile thanks to the rich volcanic nutrients from the island's origin. A constant mist and spray of rain, and there grows a lush green landscape in no time, especially with no indigenous rodents or predators. Aunt Maude surely knew how to dart her thoughts in the right direction.

'This whole plantation is a haven for lone women, look at your mistress, she needs a man, I tell you, *par le nom de Dieu*, how can a woman run a plantation on her own?!' The lines of her frown relaxed, her eyes sparkled, the severity of her lips spread into a smile.

'It would be nice to marry you off to Tonton Fanfan's nephew, and find a suitor for Madame.' In a move to approach the young girl holding the baby, the old Aunt let out a sigh ... *'tick tick, ayo bon dieu'* her way to click her tongue and show that there was little hope while imploring God for an answer.

Claw-like fingers closed around Veronique's forearms as she pulled her down. What could she do? She let herself be pulled in, leaned down and reluctantly pressed her cheek to her wrinkled face. It was dry and looked like old leather, yet soft as silk to the touch; dark as mahogany, it smelt of face powder mixed with something biting, lemony, old-lady-ish. She let go of her arms, placed those scraggy hands around her face, and looked into her eyes. This time for more than a glance. Their gazes locked; hers held the young girl's one. She could not look away. These were not the eyes of a life-weary curmudgeon with one foot in the grave. Fire was in those eyes, and life; and, to her astonishment, an amused twinkle, as if she were enjoying a private joke, as if she read her through and through. Condescension fled. Veronique felt a mist of sweat form on her upper lips and wished this moment would end as soon as possible. If she could fly, she would seek her mistress and bring her back from where she was. A strange bond had set in between Devika and Veronique, not because of the baby, but of a tacit understanding of a day to day survival in this vast place. Devika even comforted her sometimes and cooked her delicious Mauritian meals, she had never tasted before, and they all had won her over. Her Aunt was quite right; Veronique wasn't much of a cook, she only did what she had seen others doing. But she was deeply and passionately learning about healthy foods. She hoped to raise the baby and serve Madame a variety of whole grains, organic vegetables and healing herbs. They both looked quite battered when they arrived and now Devika was picking a bit of colour on her cheeks. Both women would cohabit in long silences after the meals when sat under the veranda. They had been living, breathing, moving human beings, filled with life and love, moved by emotions and passions, just as aware of their own lives, and unaware that one day in the distant future a young girl carrying their love in her heart would carve her own way under the sky.

4 HOME

The absence of a man with a strong hold over the monumental tasks on the tea plantation, started to be felt. The recent cyclone had left some trees with broken branches, many uprooted, and bushes blown to the ground. It was a muddy sight everywhere; the river broke its banks and was now flowing normally but all laid bare around it. It looked desolate, the air felt thick with humidity and smelled of rotten greens. Devika didn't know where to start to reclaim back the paradise it was, when she last saw it. When she looked near the house, all the papaya trees were just stumps, with no tops, the avocado tree was naked, and the canopies of bougainvillea had dropped to the ground. Disaster had a name, Rosella it was. As mighty as a woman in wrath, islanders feared cyclones which came slowly with a pending precursor of hot and humid days.

“Madame, shall I make you tea?” asked sweet voiced Veronique.

“Yes, that’s a good idea, thank you *Ma chère*”

A good cuppa is said to heal the bruised soul. Devika suspended her thoughts for a moment and looked at the stuffed stag’s head hanging on the wall, with its glass eyes. Why was this poor dead animal hung as a trophy? She felt the agony of the animal when the bullet ripped through its vulnerable flanks. No, there was no need to display such things around the house. She told Veronique to get rid of them. There were four around the house, one on the verandah, two in the living room and one in the hallway. A vase of fresh cut flowers, and some indoor plants were all the house needed to bring in the outdoor nature inside. Not a dead animal's stuffed head.

When night fell, Veronique had already hidden away all the bits that she thought were upsetting Devika. She was a fast learner. She brought in terracotta pots, trays and lamps, had oil and wicks in them, and proceeded to light them. It felt very much like Diwali.

In the yellow glow of the oil lamp, Devika could see the lights swaying amid the wreckage of her loneliness like survivors from a storm. Mildewed books from their shelves and some blue and white china on the antique dresser – her uncle's beloved willow patterned collection stood in their quiet elegance across the shiny wooden floor. She remembered eating a splattered mess of rice and dhal with vegetables on one of those plates when she visited him when she was a little girl.

"A fried fish is always a sure way to get you to become clever my girl" her uncle would say, seeing her pushing away the fish from her plate. Devika has always had a repugnance for fish.

"It is full moon tonight; I love this time of the month when it shines brightly among the star-filled night sky. It reminds me of my mother, maybe she is looking down from where she is, you know, Madame? shall I make a fire outside, we can have *Ayapana tisane* after dinner and watch the moon." Veronique was discreet and attentive. Like an angel gliding swiftly from corner to corner to shed light.

So, it was done, and the magic of the tropical night with a full moon shining was joyous enough to dispel some of the sadness in Devika's heart. She sat watching Veronique, hunched, gleaming eyes, while she blew gently on the dying embers of the fire and added a few more sticks. As it came alive again with a crackle, the room filled with the sweet scent of camphor wood.

The balmy night turned chilly as the hours progressed and the fire was dying. This was how distinctive the high plateau on the island differed from the coast. Warm during the day, with cool breezy nights. Veronique brought a blanket for each of them and huddled in close. In the half-dark they could see the spiky rows of tea bushes cascading away down the steep slopes. Columns of ghostly smoke rose from the fires of the villages hidden in the meadowlands below. Around her, the conical, densely wooded hills of eucalyptus stood darkly against the lightening horizon. Sometimes, the tamarind tree let out a gentle psithurism to break the silence of the night.

Could life get better and fall into place just like this perfect night displayed around them? Devika certainly had a good reflective evening and pondered what would wake her tomorrow, when dawn breaks. It had better be a good start. That night, she bedded down in the box-bed but didn't sleep for the anxious thoughts that spun in her head. For the hundredth time she cursed the storm, the fallen trees and the wretched garden that had led her task to be monumental. Her husband left her before even seeing his child! The pain was suffocating. The baby moaned and cried in her sleep. She fell asleep just before dawn and dreamt of the sea at Plaines des Roches crashing onto a white beach, and her baby drawing unsteady steps dangerously close to the shore. She woke up with a fright.

She decided to take matters into hand and send an ad to the newspapers to recruit a manager for Bonne Espérance.

5 SEBASTIEN

The nine thousand six hundred and forty-six-mile journey from St. Malo to Port Louis, Ile de France, was an experience in itself. When I reached the port of embarkation, it was crowded with passengers and luggage, together with family and friends all going down to see them off. Jolly music was being played and there was a holiday atmosphere about it all, almost like a celebration, and when I saw them all enjoying themselves, I wished I had known about it beforehand so that Claire and Maman could have shared it with me. St Malo is on the North bank of the shoreline housing the port, and there was a lovely view of the docks and ships as the train took us right through into the embarkation area, where after passing through all the formalities, I boarded at 4 pm. This was the first really large ship I had ever seen, and she looked enormous as I walked up the gangway to the entrance port in her hull. Later I wrote to Maman, that the ship was as long as the local football pitch to give her a sense of size she could understand, but in actual fact, 'La Cancale' was twice as long as that. Although she looked impressive from the outside, her inside was absolutely bewildering, for she was a maze of corridors, cabins and stairways, all of which seemed identical to the uninitiated, and it was several days before I was able to find my way about, without hesitation. The decks were lettered from A to E, A being the top sports deck, from which magnificent views could be had all around the ship, while B deck contained all the public rooms, lounges, bars, shops and reading and games rooms. Below this on C deck were the first-class cabins. The deck D housed the galleys, dining rooms and more shops and restaurants, while the Tourist Class cabins were below again on E deck, very near the water line. One of the drawbacks with them was that they were very near the engines, which made them extremely noisy.

Once aboard I discovered Berth No. 226 with some difficulty and found that I was in a two-berth cabin which I was to share with a lad named Bill Stones. He was on his maiden journey like me to Ile de France. He was from Bristol, born to a French mother, so he spoke Molière's language fluently. It made the voyage more pleasant as we could converse and share our apprehensions of reaching to a new country totally unaware of any of its people, culture or climate. Except that we only knew that it was a tropical island and had nice beaches, besides where we shall be stationed.

The cabin was nicely furnished with separate beds, a small wardrobe and dressing table each, and also a porthole. After an hour or so, we heard over the last call for all those visitors who were not sailing to go ashore, so we went up on deck to see our departure. Although it was dark by now, the landing stage was a blaze of lights, and there was pandemonium as we cast off at 5.30 pm amid a bedlam of noise, people shouting, whistling and cheering to each other, klaxons screeching and a suitable march being played over the ship's loudspeakers. However, gradually we edged away from the quay into the January darkness, and within minutes we were in midstream and then started slipping away down the bright shoreline with lights twinkling.

The journey had begun.

During the first few days of the voyage there was a rather strange atmosphere on the ship, as we were hundreds of complete strangers getting to know each other and trying to discover like-minded people we could be friendly with until we reached our destinations. As I had never travelled before, at that time I was rather withdrawn and didn't find talking to strangers very easy. Initially, when I listened to some of the other passengers talking, I was amazed at the number of what I thought were British on board. During the war, we had had many American troops stationed in St Malo, but I had never heard nor seen so many British at one time. The weather was good for the first 400-mile, but as we rounded the French coast near Brest and then started to cross the Bay of Biscay, I half expected all sorts of wild things to happen. Once you leave Brittany and head for Cape Finistère, you have left the comparatively shallow waters of the Continental Shelf behind and are then crossing the depths of the Atlantic Ocean proper. The adventure had just begun, in my head, I conjured monsters threatening to rise from the depths of the ocean in the Jules Verne style, and storms to rock the ship as a bouncing castle.

As the La Cancale did the voyage regularly I knew there was nothing to worry about, but I did expect to see some noteworthy waves, and was a little disappointed when all we got was a bit of a roll from a choppy sea that made some of us feel just a little bit queasy. The letter of employment I received was signed by a woman, so what would this boss lady of mine be like? All of this apprehension only contributed to making my stomach churn even more.

We didn't get to bed until 3 am chatting away, but the morning bell woke us as usual at 7 am, and because it looked like a lovely, sunny morning through the porthole, I hurriedly shaved and dressed and quickly went out on deck, to be met by an absolutely breathtakingly beautiful sight. The sun was shining through a cloudless deep cerulean blue sky, while the slightly jade blue Mediterranean was as still as a pond, and the ship was sailing along a few miles out from the North African coast near Algiers. The air felt balmy with a burnt smell. It was a lovely pale brown and rosy pink colour in the early morning sun, and the cliffs atop the deserted ragged shoreline was visible like a mirage. This beautiful pink landscape, reflected in the sea as though in a mirror, was suspended between the two shades of blue, a really unforgettable sight, much unlike what was usually seen in St Malo. I felt elated for no reason, but surely the landscape was to do with it. It was one of those sights which leave an imprint, forever in our minds to become cherished memories later. I know that this journey will end well. I just knew it.

We moored in Port Said harbour at 6 am on a Saturday and it was an absolute revelation to me. The winter sun was already very hot, and from our moorings in the outer harbour I got a good view of the city and the hundreds of ships and small boats that were plying their trade around the harbour and the larger vessels that were waiting their turn to pass through the Suez Canal. This was the very first glimpse I had ever had of a foreign city, and I was looking forward to going ashore to see the sights after our formalities had been completed. But we were told that we cannot go further than the main gate of the docks. Many passengers preferred to lean against the sides of the decks and look down. No outsiders were allowed on board the ship, so all the other local traders conducted their business from countless small 'bum-boats' which thronged around her. They were packed with all sorts of goods and local produce, from leather items, stools, bags, shoes and clothing to Egyptian sweetmeats, postcards, fruit and models of the pyramids. These were sent up for inspection in wicker baskets tied to cords which were tossed up to the upper decks, then after inspection and bargaining they were either returned the same way or the money was sent down. Considering the number of ships which were waiting to pass through the canal, the water in the harbour was remarkably clear, and small boys swam near the stern of the ship to dive for coins which were tossed from the upper decks. They were like eels in the water, and there were very few coins which weren't snapped up by them before they sank too deep to be collected.

That night, the rest of the canal was negotiated with the help of searchlights mounted on the bridge, and morning found us in the Gulf of Suez. Although it is roughly 180 miles long, the Gulf is less than 25 miles wide for most of its length, with desert and mountains on both shores, and as we passed through the southern Straits into the Red Sea we got a clear view of Mount Sinai of biblical fame along with its white monastery. In comparison, the Red Sea is about 150 miles wide, but why it was named the Red Sea remains a mystery, for here the water was of an ultramarine blue. My take on it is the theory that there was a typo mistake in the bible. Instead of reed, it was spelled red. Research has shown that the time of the escape of the Israelites from Egypt coincides with the period when a gigantic volcanic eruption destroyed the island of Thera, or Santorini in the Eastern Mediterranean, and the gigantic tsunami wave it generated was so devastating that the great city of Knossos, many miles inland on the island of Crete was destroyed and the Minoan civilization was brought to an abrupt end. This could have been one of many such waves, and from Egyptian records it is recorded that the narrow neck of land that connects the Mediterranean with the Gulf of Suez was very low lying in those days, and consisted of swamps and boggy land on which vast beds of reeds grew, and was known as the Reed Sea. It was across this swamp that the Israelites would have had to cross to escape from Egypt, and the theory has been formulated that this could have coincided with the retreat of the waters from the land due to the first action of a tsunami, which allowed them to cross safely, and then flooded again when the Egyptian army tried to follow them.

Most of the evening entertainment on board after dinner seemed to finish at about midnight, and instead of going straight to bed,

I would often go up on the Sports deck and stand for a while, taking in some fresh air and assimilating the beauty of the night. In good weather, the sky was a dark, velvet blue, in which the stars seemed to twinkle and shine much more clearly and brightly than they did at home. Experiencing the mystique of being on a lone ship in the middle of thousands of square miles of empty ocean, I can quite understand why some deep-water sailors find it very hard to settle down on shore after a lifetime at sea. The voyage gave me very long hours to meditate upon what was awaiting me on that island.

While crossing the Indian Ocean the weather was superb, with just a heavy swell which made the ship roll at times. Her air-conditioning and forced ventilation were fine, so we had no difficulty in doing all our packing in order to be ready for going ashore the next day. However, it was hot enough to make us realise that without these artificial aids it would have been unbearably hot inside the ship. My thoughts went to the shiploads of slaves caught, sold and boarded to unknown lands, far away, held by colonial masters. One such ship would have sailed to Mauritius, where I was heading to. I couldn't stop feeling a strange sensation in my stomach, inferring all the atrocities which may have accompanied the slaves on their fearful journeys. And here I was going about visiting new places, playing games, having air conditioning, mountains of pastries and endless coffee to keep with the long hours on board.

6 ZANZIBAR

When La Cancale slid into the dock, the sun was burning down and the cool ocean breezes were now behind them.

Sébastien loved to feel the sun on his skin – the heat was like food to him, nourishing, burning the life back into his body from where it had been drained away by the cold gloom of the Atlantic battering his homely coast of Finistère. He breathed deeply, drawing the warm marine air into his lungs, savouring the smell of the land after weeks at sea. Standing on the foredeck, Sébastien watched the sea birds circling the boats and dhows scattered around the bay. They were ready to swoop and dive hungrily to the surface of the water to scoop up any scraps of food thrown by the fishermen. Ahead, the land throbbed with heat and, under the distorting haze of the sun, the port was a vibrant splash of primary colours, as brown-skinned bearers carried sacks of produce from the mainland. Huge bales of bright-hued fabrics and baskets overflowing with tropical fruits and spices.

Indian almond trees with their large leafy crop gave more shade than an umbrella, to women draped in bright bold patterned fabrics, sometimes with a baby hanging behind, on their back. Sébastien could smell the rich aroma of those spices in the air, mingling with the tang of salt from the ocean and the sharpness of sweat from the procession of labouring men as they carried produce between ships and warehouses. It took several hours to partially unload the Cancale of the cargo designated for Zanzibar and replenish her hold.

She was a tramp steamer on a long circular voyage, picking up and depositing cargo as she went, in a series of short runs along the way. She followed no regular route, but went where the loads were, discharging one cargo and seeking a replacement. Her cargo changed constantly, depending on the port, everything from sugar, salt and spices to scrap metal and machine parts.

This would be only a brief stopover – the ship would sail on the first tide next morning, not long after dawn, but until midnight they were free to enjoy the sights and sounds of Zanzibar, to explore its bazaars, drink their fill in its quayside bars, and sample the delights of its spicy cuisine. The ground on the dockside underfoot was hot as a gridiron. Prostitutes were evident everywhere, calling out to the men as they swaggered by, knowing the sailors could have been weeks at sea without the comfort and pleasure of a woman's body. Some men succumbed, peeling away from the group, happily led by the hand by smiling white-toothed women with skin like burnished ebony. Sébastien never gave them a second glance. He drifted in the narrow alleys with beautifully carved doors in timber, each one could easily win its place in a museum for their sheer intricate carving. Also called Gujarati doors, because they are made by merchants and craftsmen from Surat, they are usually divided into smaller sections and have foldable shutters. Some have heavy brass studs and arched top frames, just like in Indian palaces. Brass studs came from India, where they were used to protect the doors against elephants. The carved decorations generally showcase the wealth of the resident with various ornaments and patterns.

Wave-like patterns and ropes allude to seaborne trade. Chains are said to protect the building from evil spirits, but they also mark the mansions of wealthy Arab slave traders. Flowers at the top of the door tell how many families used to live inside, whereas vines refer to the spice trade. Geometric shapes, like squares, refer to accountants. Sébastien caught up with this local information when he stopped at a roadside cafe to quench his thirst with a chilled fresh juice. The cafe owner was chatty and wanted to practice his English, but found that Sebastien was French, although this still didn't deter him. He carried on talking, and Sebastien could pick what he was saying relying upon his high school English. Apart from that, cats were abundant, and the place looked dead.

He found a brightly lit bar which was buzzing, the food and drink accompanied by live jazz music – the singers handpicked by the owner for the beauty of their faces more than for the melody of their voices. Tonight, there was a mixed crowd at the tables, mostly men: crews from other ships, merchants and traders, British and German settlers in Zanzibar to do business, assorted consular officials of varying nationalities, the odd policeman and, this evening, a table of four Germans, two of them in naval uniform and sporting the sinister-looking band on their upper arm - where once there would have been a visible swastika.

Sébastien ordered some grilled seafood which came with rice and *kachumbari*, a Swahili name for a cucumber and tomato salsa with hot chilies. Some chilled beer washed the heat down his burning throat, and he stayed drinking till late, listening to the loud music. Next morning, he woke and went straight away to the deck. He looked out over the roofs of the city. On some of the nearby buildings he could see women already up and putting their washing on the flat rooftops, in the half-light before the sun rose fully and made working more arduous. His head was pounding, his mouth raw and his stomach upset – the delayed penalty for the combination of cheap beer and spicy food. Stone Town, laid in front of him, looking bored and hot, steeped in time which looked like it stood still. He had read so many exciting things about Zanzibar and it was a shame that he didn't have enough time to explore it. He wanted to know more about this place as it had a huge connection to the island of Mauritius, where he was heading. Most slaves were shipped from here by the French to work on their estates. The same dock which is now holding this ship he is on; he would have a different destiny to the slave who was chained and thrown in those horrendous ships at that time.

The dockside was deserted but the deck of the Cancale was a hive of activity as the crew made ready for departure. The hatches were closed, cargo checked, derricks secured, the steam already up, and the crew were everywhere checking everything moveable was safely stowed, the gangway was lifted, and the moorings were slipped. The horn sounded and the ship eased away from the quay. For days, the voyage had no halt, it was straight sailing, and the weather was very good. A vastness of blues above and beyond which merged into each other, blurring the horizon line, giving the allusion that all that existed was the sky and the ocean.

7 PORT LOUIS

The moment I woke the next morning, I sensed that something was different, so for a few seconds I laid still, gathering my thoughts. Then, I realised what it was. The engines had stopped. For the first time, in two weeks the ship was as silent and steady as a floating hotel. Ever since we had left St Malo, I was lying in my bed without feeling the movement and vibrations of a ship at sea, so she must have sailed quietly into our berth and moored up. It was a strange feeling to be back to normality, without the motion. We were soon to disembark and touch firm land for good. The voyage had come to an end. I gathered my stuff, had a wash, got ready and grabbed my bag to find my way to the exit. When I reached the deck, a peaceful cerulean blue sky greeted me.

After disembarking and completing the formalities at the customs desk, I looked around me to see any recognisable face. But there was none. Of course, in my silly thinking, I expected to see some familiar faces in an unknown country. What struck me was the cool morning, it was none of the sweltering heat I was expecting from a tropical island. The place was neither crowded nor bustling, just some carriers helping unloading boxes and moving the stored luggage. In a similar way to St Malo, the stones around were grey, except here they were blacker and of basaltic nature. The morning air was crisp and the sky incredibly blue. I hung around the customs hall for a while collecting my thoughts, and then as nobody seemed to take the slightest bit of notice of me, I decided to go outside on the street passing the huge wrought iron gate next to an imposing grey stone building which was a Post office. A few people were waiting there, with some women with umbrellas. Some had taken shade under two huge banyan trees. By their laid-back attitude, they seemed that their waiting was comfortable enough.

I had been told that someone would pick me up, so I started looking around for some kind of recognition of a name being called or a board displaying my name. Nothing. I waited for half an hour. A small tap on my shoulder made me turn around to a surprising vision. A petite brunette with soft features, gleaming brown eyes, dressed in a white organdie saree with a lace blouse was smiling at me.

'Sébastien Laval? She uttered in an equally soft voice.

'*Oui, c'est moi!*'

'*Je suis Devika, de Bonne Espérance, soyez le*

bienvenu.'

Here we go, someone has come to collect me. But how did this pretty lady know me? I was still searching for an answer when she made it easy for me by saying with a wide smile, flashing some incredulous white teeth,

'I thought I might not recognise you, as we had forgotten to exchange photos, but the newspaper helped by sending me your application for the job, as they had your photo on file. Besides, you do look French, like many of the passengers coming from France on board this ship. Did you have a good trip?'

'I see, yes, it was very good, we had several stops and I enjoyed discovering places I had only read about in books.'

We were walking down a large open space where an avenue, lined with tall palm trees, came to an intersection of streets, then I heard and saw the bustle of what the city really was.

'That's what's good about long travels. Bhai Habib, the driver, is waiting for us nearby.'

A car suddenly came up to us. A chalk blue Morris minor, with an affable looking guy with a deep furrowed brow and a large smile with impeccable white rows of teeth. Everyone seems to have healthy and bright teeth here, I thought, that's a good sign. This should not match with the reality of an island of sugar cane.

My suitcase and hand luggage were loaded in the back, and I took a seat by the driver.

'Bonjour Monsieur, soyez le bienvenu à l'île Maurice. Moi, c'est Bhai Hamid.'

'Bonjour, merci, je suis Sébastien. Ravi de faire votre connaissance.'

The rest of the trip saw us exchanging some details of my travel, and the countries where we stopped. Devika handed me a bottle of chilled water and some bananas. She kept quiet for the rest of the journey. The tropical lushness was new to me and looked very fresh and green. Even greener than late Spring in St Malo. I didn't feel tired, but my eyes were heavy, and I was feeling drowsy. We finally reached the tea estate, I immediately recognized it by the rows of green bushes of tea lined neatly as far as the eyes could reach. A slight mist filled the air, and it was pleasantly cool.

The house appeared after a bend by a pond, and it looked grand. I was expecting a small stone house. But this was as large as a farm in Brittany, with tiled roofs and elegant windows. The place was spotless. What was I expecting? Each sight exploded a bubble in my imagination, steeped in stereotypes. I had projected the place to be unlike what unfurled in front of me, delightfully welcoming. I was sure this is a place I could spend the rest of my lifetime in, then reality shook me, and made me stand up. My job was for a probation period of 6 months, after which if I performed well, I could be offered a permanent position.

I was greeted by a blushing pretty girl by the name of Veronique who showed me the way to my room. Devika bid me a good rest and to see me for dinner. In a brightly lit room with tall windows and calico curtains, red polished wooden floors, a small double bed with clean white sheets under a billowing tent of mosquito netting bestowed a warm welcome to me. I was wide-eyed and sleepless, to the sounds of the early afternoon invading the room on a warm perfumed breeze.

An armchair upholstered in mocha cream canvas, was in a corner, besides a well-polished mahogany desk and chair, some wall shelves with books and a vase with freshly cut flowers by the bedside table. Clean towels were neatly kept on my bed, and Veronique told me that the bathroom was down the corridor on the right, I couldn't miss it as there was a sign on the door saying *'salle de Bain'*

'Bienvenu à Bonne Espérance Monsieur Sebastien!' On this, she discreetly closed the door and disappeared.

8 AT THE TEA ESTATE

Sébastien had a quick shower and changed his clothes which smelled of sweat and dust. He wondered whether Devika was already downstairs waiting for him to join for dinner. He looked at himself in the oval gilded mirror hanging by the door, the reflection was that of a medium height man with sharp features, deep set green eyes, auburn hair with golden tips and a happy looking face with laughter lines. Working for a tea estate seemed like a great unknown adventure. He believed that his training in farms across Brittany, after his degree, would be sufficient to shoulder his new job's challenge. However, it still felt a bit daunting. He wondered how he was chosen for this job.

The heat gradually peaked by midday, making everyone more languid. Drab, grey St Malo was just a distant memory. The days here were filled with sunshine, the relentless blue of the sky and the shimmering, endless sea in the far distance as a line of ultramarine and turquoise. Devika had explained to Sébastien what she expected of him at the tea estate. He had quickly come to terms with the tea plantation essentials, the foremen gave him some indications of the tropical weather and its effects on the growth of the young shoots and buds which will turn into delicious tea once smoked and dried.

Settling into a routine, established by Devika and Veronique, time after dinner was taken with a tisane on the verandah. Sitting in deckchairs under the clear sky, with a large blanket of stars, spending the evening discussing plans to bounce Bonne Espérance back to life again.

Some nights, the hills were at first a blue smudge on the horizon shrouded in tropical mists, like mystical kingdoms from a storybook, then a silvery moon would punch through until the clouds gave it a pinkish halo. Veronique would say, it predicted a rainy and dull day.

Sébastien was adjusting to the laidback tropical pace of working without losing at any task assigned to him. Devika, though warm and polite, was never beyond her professional self. She looked forlorn at times and would avoid any eye contact. Then the expression would vanish, replaced by the brisk efficiency that characterised her.

Sébastien wanted to unlock the door of mystery that surrounded his new boss. She was as charming as she could be at one moment yet closed as a carp the next. Devika was not only the lovely creature he first saw at the harbour but a woman far lovelier when he caught glimpses of her history as to how she landed becoming the mistress of Bonne Espérance. Véronique, who never missed an exchange of conversation with him, would rush to give him more information than he asked for.

He waited to be alone with Devika to draw closer to her, but the opportunity never arose. Where Devika was, Veronique was never far away.

Sébastien's amazement of the grounds of the house grew each day, as he discovered and learnt new plants and their names. The whole was bordered by a dense and dripping forest foliage of huge banana trees with wide leaves, palm fronds, creepers and vines, mosses and ferns. Yellow-beaked mynah birds chattered among the trees, flocks of sparrows came to peck at the broken rice grains Veronique fed them each afternoon. There were mango trees, flame trees, papaya trees, breadfruit trees, cinnamon trees, yellow-flowered cassia, big lilac jacaranda, throngs of hibiscus with red flowers shaped like little cups, feathery casuarina trees that whispered in the wind, the tall jasmine creeper with creamy-white flowers that smelled wonderful after rain, as well as the sweet-scented frangipanis that grew all over the island. He loved the tiger yellow and red canna lily flowers, the golden jackfruit, the tall clumps of feathery bamboo, ripe black jamuns, hedges of bright-pink and purple bougainvillea scrambling over trellises, the smell of the curry leaves and lemon grass, which was often served as an infusion with fresh root ginger. Yellow cardinals, canaries, red *lall Moonias*, dove turtles fluttered around every morning and evening, ready to be fed.

On some evenings, when it was chillier, Veronique lit a fire in a pit. She would spend her time tending to the flames, adding more sticks and moving the embers around. Sébastien tried several times to chat up Devika, but she was her usual, quiet self.

He looked at Devika again, whose face was glowing by the flames she was intensely looking at, as if mesmerized and drilling into a far memory, as she parted her lips to eat a biscuit, he felt another rush of blood to his head and a desperate desire to kiss her. He'd never felt a compulsion to kiss a woman before. He didn't even know her. And yet he felt he did. It was if he had always known her. Now that she was sitting here opposite him, he knew he wanted her always to be sitting close to him like that. Was it the exotic environment to blame? Finistère felt very far, and cold.

*

Tea rivalled sugar cane, after a priest, Father Galloys introduced it to the island. Pierre Poivre planted it on a large scale in 1770. But, till the advent of the British, it remained little more than a museum plant. In the 19th century, Robert Farquhar, Governor of

Mauritius, encouraged commercial tea cultivation. He had a tea garden at Le Réduit. Unfortunately, when he left Mauritius, the plantation was abandoned, as no one was interested in his scheme. Seventy years later, Sir John Pope Hennessy revived local interest in tea cultivation and consequently tea plantation was started at Nouvelle France and at Chamarel. Plantations were established and by the end of the century, 190 hectares had been planted. Gradually, more people became interested in tea cultivation and there was a net increase in private plantations and new factories were built. By World War II, 850 hectares were under tea, five factories had been established and production for local consumption was in full swing.

This new crop on the island made a side economy for the sugar planters and they revelled in the joys of sipping the brew at all times of the day. The Chinese concoction was brought to India, and there they developed crops with good yields with full bodied flavours. Later, they found out that there were other varieties which were indigenous to the region. That came as a bonanza. They were cultivated and brought a large profit for the East India Company. These same cultivars were brought and tried with success on the island. It was a bit capricious, and didn't like too much warmth, but excelled on the high plateau of the island where a constant frequent mist and cool temperature suited the tea shrubs very well. They remain verdant on gentle slopes, where the air constantly smelled clean and fresh.

Devika could never have enough watching the green expanses reaching till as far as the eyes could see, with a small pride swelling in her.

"I own this!" She thought with gratefulness.

She needed to go over the books with Sébastien and have a good strategy to cut down costs and renew the crops. The young man has been zealous about learning from all sources he could, and never missed a chance to discuss fresh ideas with her. He had this almost juvenile twinkle in his eyes when he spoke, that made Devika feel protective about him. She was very hopeful that with his talent Bonne Espérance will be in good hands.

*

The sun was watery and yellow, rising over the treetops, the air fresh and smelling of eucalyptus and damp earth. Devika closed her eyes and breathed it in.

'Best part of the day, isn't it?'

Startled, she spun round. Sébastien was standing in white shirt and khaki trousers, hair still ruffled from sleep, smiling at her. Her stomach lurched. She did not like to show this vulnerable side of herself.

'Yes,' she agreed, pushing loose, unbrushed hair behind her ears, self-conscious at her own dishevelled state at this early moment of the morning.

'I didn't think anyone would be up. I thought I'd walk ... couldn't sleep.' 'Can I come with you?' he asked.

'Of course, I will just get changed and join you.' She nodded.

She felt a bit nervous sometimes around the young man. He was so handsome and gentle that her heart skipped a beat each time she caught her eyes on him when he was not looking. She loved his clear blue eyes' and when his pupils enlarged when explaining something to her.

What was happening to her? Months ago, she was wetting her pillow each night with nonstop tears. From the unexpected abandonment by her husband. She vowed no man will ever touch her heart again. And there she was now, growing new hopes, cautiously, over a painful heartbreak. Each time she nursed and played with her daughter, her soul would feel so happy and sad at the same time. She wondered if her husband missed seeing and knowing his child. Did paternal instinct kick his flanks with remorse? It felt as if he lived in a faraway land where she and her daughter would never reach. The brutal severance of their relationship was still unbelievable to be true. What will she tell her daughter when she grows up and asks about her father? Many questions ran into Devika's mind and scorched her heart like a hot iron marking her flesh. Life was playing queer tricks on her, she felt confused and peaceful at the same time. The vast green expanse of Bonne Espérance had a lot to do with calming her emotions, bringing some balance. She was offered hope at this stage in her life.

Now, this young stranger who has entered her daily routine is turning her feelings around, and she started hearing herself hum at times. Was the heart getting lighter with the passing days, and challenges to be met with strength and passion? There was a gentle knock at the door, which was half open.

'Come in'

'Bonjour Madame, are you going out? I came to ask you about breakfast. Should I make fried eggs this morning?' said Veronique excitedly.

'Yes, that would be nice. I am going for a short stroll with Sébastien. He is waiting outside. I shall have breakfast when I come back, after my shower, as usual. Can you please make some fresh watermelon juice today?'

'He's handsome, isn't he?' Véronique said shyly, twirling her straggly curly hair, her eyes fixed on the open window. Sébastien was hovering around the steps leading to the veranda.

'I suppose so,' Devika said, gingerly touching the side of her temple. She always did that when a little embarrassed.

'Well, I think he's very handsome,' Véronique

said. 'He's just the sort of man I'd like to marry one day.' Devika turned and laughed in surprise.

'Really?'

'Yes, really.' Said a blushing Véronique.

'Except it's obvious he's taken a fancy to you.'

'Don't be ridiculous,' Devika exclaimed.

'In fact, I know he has ... but I like him whatever you say. And maybe one day, when I'm fully grown up, he'll care about me too.'

The young man was waiting outside, ready for a walk. Devika wrapped a light shawl around her shoulders and joined him. They both stayed silent, enjoying the birds chirping away, and nature waking up at its own pace with its wild and various noises filling the air.

'Perhaps tomorrow you would like to see around our estate? The gardens are flourishing, and we produce a very delicate, superior tea. I shall take you to the area where our centennial cultivars are, they are our pride. This is from where all the tea shrubs come from.'

'What developments are there on the other tea estates, do you know?' Sébastien asked. She did not know much but was enthusiastic about mechanization and updating new machines they could install for drying and rolling the leaves.

'It's the way forward,' he agreed.

'Economies of scale and mass production.' 'But there will always be a demand for the more delicately flavoured tea,' Devika countered, 'that is grown at higher altitude and picked by hand, early in the season.'

'Maybe – if the estate is well run. But so many of the smaller ones have gone to the wall because they are just too costly, and their practices are inefficient.'

'Such as?' Sébastien frowned.

'The system of labour, you need workers on the spot all year round, not coming and going with the seasons when it pleases them or when the harvest is bad.'

'Now, that's where you fill in, find us that magical formula that this tea estate is brought back to life.'

'The trees you got replanted; they're growing haphazardly all over the hillside – the way the Chinese grow them. You should have terracing and they should be much closer together; more bushes, more leaves, more profit. And the soil's all wrong up here – not sandy enough.'

'Sandy soil up here? Are you mad? We are far from the coast although you can see it from around the bend. What has sand got to do with tea?'

'Sand ensures good drainage. Most of the fields which are new need to get the soil reworked, sand brought in and mixed. Then, things can improve. As for the processing; it's archaic!

You still have a shed full of men rolling leaves by hand. You'll never be cost-effective. The only way you can save your estate from ruin is to amalgamate with the big estates so you can use the modern machinery and change your practices.'

Devika sparked back. 'Bonne Espérance has a future – when we can find someone with the imagination to see how special it is and the drive to do more than just criticise. I thought you might be such a man,' she said with a look of admiration. They discussed that they must turn around the fortunes of Bonne Espérance. They needed an injection of capital to see them through the lean time before the new trees fully matured. A financial backer. How to find one?

They walked back to the house and parted with good spirits, ready to attack the long day with aplomb. The hill and the wood were coming alive with some distant noises. Feeling energetic from the walk, Devika swiftly dressed in her best casual saree, a hand-me-down of her mother's, of peach-coloured Japanese voile with a thin border. She carefully brushed out her long hair and arranged it in a neat plait. Thoughts of Sébastien kept coming to her mind. He was new to Mauritius and still finding his feet. It began to dawn on her that he might be useful to her, more than she expected. He breathed of honesty and was a quick learner. There was so much passion in his talks. This gave Devika hope that she had indeed recruited the right person, for Bonne Espérance.

9 BHAI HAMID

The period of hot days arrived unseasonably warmer than usual, without the early light drizzle that brought forth the delicate first tea buds. The tea pickers picked what they could, but the agents from Bourbon frowned and grumbled over the stock they received and offered very little for its worth. The leaves of the tea bushes grew sparsely and too small. They waited in vain for proper rains to start. ‘Winter will come soon,’ predicted Tonton Marcel, the old keeper, ‘if it is God’s will, we might have some rain then.’

In the village, they offered puja at the nearby

kalimaye to the gods to send rain, for the nearby reservoir's water level had gone down. The usual fishermen on the sloping banks of the reservoir, have been left as a bunch of stragglers. The carps, and tilapias had gone deeper to keep cool and didn't paddle their way furiously to their silly death at the baits on the fishing lines.

Words and foreign phrases rioted through Sébastien's head. Créole, Bhojpuri, French patois, Bhojpuri Créole, English, Tamil. Bonne Espérance tea estate was surrounded by small hamlets and villages nestled where sugar cane fields took a step aside to let men claim their corner too, in this tiny, lush island. Impressions of a world far from the one Sébastien knew. Where he came from, hamlets were mainly granite houses, farms and barns which looked dark and dull in Winter. Where the chimneys spat puffs of smoke reminders of the need to keep people warm when the harsh winds blew Eastwards from the Atlantic sea.

Where the eroded carved out sharp abers, and gorges, in the north, made the coastline deeply indented. Where menhirs and dolmens stood facing time in a defiance. Here, the world was colourful, and Winters felt like Summers on a cool morning. Sparkling opalescent waters of Souillac Bay stretching across the Tropic of Capricorn making itself known and held in man's awe. Names and places on a map, places he never dreamed he would see. Sun. Heat. Throngs of people, darker skinned, wearing brighter colours, some draped in sarees, others in skirts and light cotton tops. The people in the tropics in this land south of the Indian Ocean speaking unfamiliar languages. Yet, he felt at home. It couldn't be from only the warmth that was offered to him since his arrival, nor the attention and care Véronique showed him, no, it was something else. Devika? The young man's mind wandered over matters that had touched him in an awkward way. It was better left to time to provide the answers.

After discussion with Devika, he had managed to convince the latter to visit her solicitor in the city to ask for legal advice regarding investors. So, they set out on the trip, early morning, after a simple breakfast of papaya, baguette, butter and jam with freshly brewed tea, and of course, coffee for Sébastien. The young man had not got used to drinking tea even while working for a tea estate. It somehow had not yet settled to his palate, him liking his strong caffeine to start the day. They left the house and took a detour to avoid the morning rush hour, Sébastien could not peel his eyes off the new landscape unfurling in front of him. Many unexpected views announced themselves as they turned tight corners: a wall overlooking a ravine covered in *'la liane lang'* as the driver uttered, serving as guide to Sébastien. A church clinging to its side in deep black basalt blocks and a cock on its spire; falls of bougainvillea, sparrows taking a bath at a hand fountain, splashing water poured from the urn of a statue into a big aluminium pail; patches of dark shadow, patches of bright light, dappled ground around the trees. Birds singing from their perches on flagpoles jutting over secret squares; mango trees laden with fruits of all shapes he had never seen. Naively, he thought they existed in only one variety. He had seen them appearing during Christmas in supermarkets in Finistère. Christmas on Mauritius would herald fresh lychees with their clusters hanging heavily nearly touching the ground.

For now, Papaya trees hold their oblong ripening fruits close to the main trunk while their wide fan-like leaves seem to provide a shelter from the hot sun. Yellow Cuscutes covered many tall bushes in their parasitic clutches.

They passed by a river where some women were washing clothes on a bare large rock by the banks leaving a white froth in the flow of the water. Some waved while putting their washing along lines made from aloe poles tied with coconut coir. It was customary to do the laundry by the river, as there was no regular running water in the smaller hamlets, but it was also an escape to the outdoors while catching up on the latest gossip and news within the community. The women thrived on these networks to get on with their lives, which had many restrictions.

They reached the city, while Sébastien'e eyes remained glued on the outside, in amazement. Colonial buildings and houses, restaurants were stacked tightly against one another; twisting small cobbled paved streets barely wide enough for two people to walk side by side; small shops with men huddled in for a fag, in the wait for their official paperwork to be carried out by busy legal offices. Carnations and pelargoniums planted in old Indian ghee tins spilled red flowers like spots of blood while pink wild roses climbed trellises on the balconies of the buildings. Many were inhabited by the locals. It was a dual lifestyle, one being domestic, the other official.

'Most of the houses you see above the shops are inhabited by Muslims traders. They are Surtis, a group of traders who came to the island from Surat in Gujarat, India, to seek their fortune. They tended not to mix with the rest of the other Muslims as they regard them as of low caste and class. As a result, they marry only within family groups and many of their progeny are often born with disabilities, due to inbreeding. They keep to their traditions and make natural essential oils from their homegrown roses and geraniums,' Devika explained to Sébastien. They arrived at a small but packed parking lot, where Bhai stopped. Devika and Sébastien got down, happy to stretch their legs.

'Right,' Devika said. 'Let's get this over and done with.' After turning many small streets, they reached a white colonial building with tall louvred shutters. A bronze metallic plaque read the solicitor's name.

Devika raised her finger and pressed the buzzer. The door opened and in they went. They found themselves in an air-conditioned reception area, with swathes of glossy wood and butter-soft dark leather furniture. Birds of paradise and red anthurium blooms stood proud above an enormous glass vase beside the desk. They introduced themselves and the bespectacled busy looking receptionist invited them to take a seat, which they did; sitting awkwardly side by side. A few minutes later, the solicitor's assistant came and invited them to follow her into a tiny, dark mirrored lift. Sébastien held his breath and pressed his hands against the wall behind him to prevent any part of his body touching Devika. The lift was slow and cranky and smelled of reams of paper from a printer. They could hear the clink of typewriters outside as the lift doors closed behind them.

The lawyer, Me Noel, was waiting for them in a room on the first floor. He spoke fluent English and French, was courteous and his tone was kindly; he put them at ease. His office looked grand with large law books in their shiny lettered hardbacks. There was a jug of water on the table and several upturned glasses. Sébastien filled one and drank the water, after offering one to Devika. The small walk in the hot humid city had made him long for a good glass of cold water to quench his thirst. He spilled some drops onto the highly polished table. The spots glared back. He quickly wiped the desktop with the underside of the cuff of his shirt. It left a smear on the wood. The assistant leaned over and passed him a paper towel, while his cheeks burnt hot with embarrassment. Why was he feeling so nervous? Obviously, it was all to do with his recommendation to Devika, and the thought of what advise Me Noel will give.

After some polite exchanges of small talk, the tone changed, and the formalities began. At this stage, the solicitor took the time to explain what was in peril if an alliance was to happen and its benefits too. Every so often, a document was placed in front of them to consult, and soon it was all over. They shook hands and exited the office, both feeling they needed some fresh air to avoid gasping at all this formal air which crushed their breathing.

'*Ah! Mais c'est ridicule*!' Devika let out first, her face was flushed, Sébastien knew it wasn't from the heat outside.

'I told you of the ramifications of an alliance, now you have heard it from your legal advisor, you might start to believe me.' Sébastien hesitated but went ahead, replying to Devika. She kept quiet and carried on walking, avoiding people coming across her direction.

Back to the car, they both took their seats without any more words spoken. Devika fanned herself, drank some water, and wiped her forehead.

Bhai Hamid started the engine and lowered the

windows. He sensed the tension in the air, took off the handbrake and manoeuvred the car out of its spot. As they moved, a flock of sparrows fluttered out of a nearby banyan tree; the busy hum of the city soon faded away. Behind them, Port Louis' dockside walls basked in the golden glow of the lowering sun, soon the traffic will thicken, commuters heading back home to cooler heights outside of the city.

"I learned there are troubles of more than one kind. Some come from ahead, others come from behind. But I've bought a big bat. I'm already, you see. Now my troubles are going to have trouble with me." Dr Seuss

The devil always gives one the best deal in the worst situations.

And temptation is at the root of it. Devika was weighing down her odds of making the tea estate work without selling her soul to the devil. And Sébastien stood by her like an archangel. But the young man didn't know about his status nor effect in the coming months of her destiny. She was only too eager to get back home and hold her daughter close to her heart. Getting her strength from her, as her life was devoid of anyone else, she could count on blindly. Each day, she hoped she would receive a letter from her wretched husband. None arrived.

'Madame, excuse me, may I drop by my house on the way to give my wage to my wife please? It will take only ten minutes. This would save me coming to Baie du Tombeau again tomorrow which might take my whole half day.'

'Of course, Bhai Hamid, you can stop by' replied Devika with a smile.

Some suburban parts of Port Louis were beautiful, others were not. They passed scruffy smallholdings, small low-cost houses called 'cité', men standing in the shade of huge mango trees on beaten earth, flat scrap lands, smoking or playing cards, while little boys played with broken wheels of bicycles and played marbles. Goats roamed around the surrounding areas, their tails twitching away the flies, climbing on mounds of rocks among aloe spiked branches.

Then, the car went through an ugly industrial and retail estate, part which smelled fishy thanks to the tuna plant nearby. Every building had their base covered in red dust, as this corner was conveniently called Terre Rouge. Brightly coloured Tamil temples stood with their gods' reliefs, clad in espaliers with defiant faces, and menacing weapons up in the air. Not far, a muezzin was calling for the afternoon prayer, while the church bells of Père Laval joined in the lively cacophony. Soon, after they had driven in silence for more than ten minutes, they came upon the ridge of a wooded hill and the sea suddenly appeared into view below them, taking Sébastien by surprise. A sparkling, jewel jade green that faded into a turquoise haze at the horizon appeared as a vision, exuding a calming peaceful golden sky.

‘Wow,’ he breathed, forgetting to be surly. ‘The light,’ He said quietly. ‘I’d forgotten the light.’ Bhai Hamid slowed the car and pulled over to the side of the road allowing them to take in the vista.

‘When was the last time you were here?’ asked Bhai Hamid to Devika. ‘Twenty years, maybe.’ ‘That’s a long time.’

‘Yes.’ Devika replied pensively.

They carried on slowly, zigzagging down the side of the hill until they reached a sharp turn, the road looping around a ramshackle tin roof cottage surrounded by a higgledy-piggledy yard. Chickens were scratching the bare soil, amongst laundry hung from the branches of old trees that threw long shadows in the afternoon light.

A middle-aged woman in a headscarf sat on a step in the shade shelling peas into a colander. She peered forward as the car stopped, squinting to see better. Nearby, an old man sat on a stool in the shade of a longan tree. One hand was on the bowl of a walking stick dug into the ground beside him, the other was holding a length of plastic twine. The twine was attached to a collar worn by a small, brown and white goat that was feeding from a bucket at the old man's feet. His shoulders were hunched, his ears stuck out like bats' wings, his head was shiny, sun-burned and wrinkly, with a wisp or two of white hair.

Bhai Hamid lifted his arm and greeted him, as he turned around towards the car,

'My father, he is 89 now!

'Is that him?' Devika answered.

'*Oui Madame,* he wants to go to hajj, but we can't afford it.'

Baie du Tombeau wasn't far, Bhai Hamid went to give the wages to his wife, and soon after, appeared smiling ear to ear with a plate of something wrapped in a newspaper.

'Madame, my wife just made hot *faratas*, she's sent these to you. Véronique cannot make like these, please have them now,'

Devika inquired about the welfare of his wife and gladly took a hot farata.

'Here, have one, they are always delicious when eaten while hot' handing it to Sebastien. The young man had an amazed look on his face and took the soft *farata*, had a bite and smiled brightly.

'This is indeed very nice, please thank your wife on my behalf. It reminds me of my own home, although not so similar to our *crêpe Bretonne*, but has the same homemade warmth to it.'

They headed back, bumped around a hairpin bend and headed steeply downhill. Bhai Hamid was taking an unexpected shortcut to reach home faster, feeling guilty for having taken time from their schedule. The tarmac road had disintegrated in places and was full of potholes. The car lurched as the wheels struggled with the uneven terrain. Sébastien braced himself against the dashboard, trying to stop his body bumping. He could see the headline: “Estranged couple drown after cliff plunge”. “Breton man’s trip ends in horror”. What was he thinking of? He was used to the flat terrain of Brittany, where he lived and this small island was certainly giving him a lot of new experiences.

‘We’re nearly there.’ stuttered Bhai Hamid.

The view of a perfect concave bay opened out before them. In the far distance, the sea and sky merged in a shimmer. Closer in, the sunlight caught the tips of small, innocuous waves whose only purpose, it seemed, was to add some sparkle to the perfectly blue water that reflected the blue sky. Fishing boats were silhouetted on the waves, disappearing into the glimmer and then reappearing. Sébastien could see a swathe of white sandy beach and, beyond that, lines of villas built above the beach road and amongst the trees that covered the hill.

'This is Baie du Tombeau, *missiez* Sébastien, I grew up here, and spent my childhood days swimming like a fish. *Ah! le bon vieux temps.*'

When they reached Bonne Espérance, Sébastien was happy to get out of the car and stood beside the ticking engine, assaulted by the outside air on the high plateau, the scent was intoxicating; the deafening buzz of insects amongst the blooms. The shadows were lengthening. The sun was blazing towards the horizon, and the promise of evening hung around them. Sébastien breathed in the air perfumed by jasmine, rose, and felt like a philocalies.

He opened the iron gate with a loud clunking as the chain that held the gates together clattered to the ground. He took hold of one of the gates and heaved. It groaned monstrously and moved slowly. When the gap was wide enough, he squeezed through and stood aside making way for Devika.

He did not go directly to the house but disappeared into the gardens.

It felt strange to be alone. It was so quiet; the only sounds were the insects and the gentle splashing of water against rock from the nearby stream down the garden. The heat contained inside the wall was warm, and the sweet waft of jasmine rising, reminiscent of Devika's perfume. He was standing on a stone paved pathway, gravel beneath the soles of his leather shoes; weeds, self-seeded grasses and wildflowers growing between the small stones. On either side, shrubs and climbers tangled together. Flowers climbed through the trees, set free from their beds and their borders. Cicadas sang; birds fluttered here and there, between the branches. It was amazing to witness nature going to sleep.

He took a few steps forward, turned a corner and saw Marcel ahead of him. Fading sunlight gilded the garden. He reached up into the leaves of a guava tree and picked a fruit. He raised it to his lips and bit into it, it was still unripe, so he threw the fruit into the flowers.

'*La nature, c'est magique*' said the old caretaker. He had come to close the small entrances along the end walls to prevent trespassing.

Sébastien nodded in silence. He naturally followed the old man through alternating patches of golden sunlight and deep shade as the drive meandered to the left, then to the right. At every step, something new revealed itself; a wild creeper scrambling over a statue of Buddha or Ganesha covered in moss; a patch of bright orange zinnias; a lizard posing on a giant sundial with a crack in its centre; a huge jackfruit tree, its trunk gnarled and solid as rock with countless green spiky bulbous fruits hanging off it defying gravity. Then, at last, behind a line of topiary gone wild, masking the last entrance door.

It was locked.

A straggler pigeon startled them, rising up from amongst the undergrowth, the sound of its wings like gunshot. Sébastien walked closer to Marcel, so close that he could smell the fabric of his shirt, his skin, his sweat of the long day. The two men waded back quietly to the villa.

When the sun set, the garden plunged into darkness, without the guidance of Marcel, he wouldn't be able to see anything. He shivered, remembering the lone walks he had to do in Winter, in his hometown. Nights were so dark, and vocal too. It's always when the night is darker that noises arise more. A fruit bat fluttered its wings and flew over their heads to a nearby tree. When the villa came into view, Sébastien realised how far he had gone into the big garden surrounding the villa. The colour of the light grew even more intense; scarlet and gold bled across the sky; one last hurrah before the sun died and the villa's façade glowed red. He felt relieved that he had reached 'home'.

Marcel bid him good night and disappeared into the darkness.

Sébastien's emotions were knotted. He needed unravelling, stretching out. He needed a bath and a comfortable bed; soft pillows, space to uncurl his emotions. He entered the villa, under the smiling eyes of Veronique who probably anticipated his tiredness. The young woman showered her care over Devika and himself with a dinner which warmed the heart. They both needed that, the day they had in the sweltering heat of the capital and the detour with Bhai Hamid were enough to dig in something comforting to feel grounded and relaxed again. They ate in silence; the forks did the talking. Sometimes, silences mend unspoken aches.

At home, in Brittany, his aunt would have cooked him his favourite chicken stew with potatoes, but here it was goat meat with chayote called *chouchou* locally. It's a delicately flavoured vegetable which grew abundantly around the house, as it loves cool climes. He has started liking his evening meals as it felt like home, discovering new tastes. Veronique was always on the side, discreet but attentive, ready to serve if anything more was needed.

‘I saw you went to the end of the garden, is that so *Missiez* Sébastien?’ Véronique inquired with a deep furrowed frown.

‘Yes, indeed, I felt like I needed some space to recollect myself after the long day in the busy capital. Besides it’s a lovely garden and I have not seen all of it. I met with Marcel who showed me the end of the estate where the villa sits, it's massive!’

‘But *Missiez* S...’

‘No *Missiez* please Veronique, just Sébastien otherwise I will feel like a stranger’

‘OK Sebastien, you should not venture out when it’s dark, it can be dangerous’

‘Why?’

'Because there is the jackfruit tree there'

'So, what about the jackfruit tree? Why is it dangerous?'

'Because... maybe you will not understand, but here, we have the *'gardien la cour*, our *grand dimoune*, you know, he lives on the jackfruit tree'

'I didn't see any tree house on the jackfruit tree; besides it is impossible to build one, it's branches are full of those spiky fruits, hanging off the trunk .... Véronique,' scoffed Sébastien.

'You should not talk like this! It is important that you don't go near that tree when it's dark, I said.' The young woman was visibly upset and couldn't express what was her concern.

'Enough Vero let's eat quietly; I will explain to him after dinner. He cannot comprehend what you are trying to tell him.'

'Madame, yes, of course. I don't want him to end up with a fever tomorrow'.

Sébastien was now more intrigued. Jackfruit tree and fever don't rhyme together. What was going on? Has he not learnt enough about jackfruit in the tropical section of his horticultural tropical fruits and vegetables books? Nothing made sense to him, why did Veronique get upset. She was speaking in riddles. Later on, while taking an infusion on the verandah, Devika whispered to him, 'it's about spirits, that's what she meant.'

'Oh, I could not understand'

'Obviously, Vero could not explain it clearly to you. She cares so much about you. There is a belief here, that if one ventures late under the tree, and if the spirit crosses your path, it might 'catch' on you. And this manifests into a fever.'

'We have plenty of such old lore and superstitions in Brittany too.' Sébastien stuttered. 'Even the famous painter Gauguin painted death and spirits. We have Ankou, the king of the dead. Much feared by the folks. He protects the graveyard and the souls around it for some unknown reason and he collects the lost souls on his land.'

'Well, here, each courtyard has its own protector. People are very scared of such spirits. They even give offerings to them. Please don't mind Vero, she means well. That's all she has known. So, now you know, at night do not to venture by the jackfruit tree!' Said Devika with a small laugh. The night around them was taking over, and Sébastien retired to his room, ready to hit the bed after brushing his teeth. He slept soundly that night, without any terrifying dreams.

10 PAUL

Morning broke with an unfamiliar and unrelenting bird song from outside his window. It was a Mynah. It's equivalent would be a blackbird in Brittany. Both birds are loud and sociable, preferring to come down on the ground when they see digging happening. They are even similar to look at, the black birds looking like a very dark mynah, with the same yellowish beak. Both birds have an almost animal-like habit of scurrying about on the ground, stabbing at the leaves and bark, trying to find insects and fallen fruit.

He vaguely recalled the bumpy ride they had

yesterday. He had a long soak in the tub last night, ridding himself of several days' sweat and a blissful night's sleep in a bed covered with a white mosquito net. This morning, like most mornings announced a fairly blue sky with broken clouds scurrying across and patterned into mackerel belly stripes. He got up and went to brush his teeth. He heard a knock and knew it was Veronique. He saw that a tray had been placed on a wicker stool beside his bed and that she was pouring him a cup of tea.

'*Bonjour Sébastien, du thé*?' greeted Veronique, while placing the cup on the bedside table. Then she pulled the curtains open and left. A groggy Sébastien sipped the tea, which was milky with a hint of vanilla, strong and delicious.

'Probably freshly manufactured as well as freshly brewed,' he thought to himself. He wondered what time it was. Feeling a little more alert, he walked over to the French windows that opened onto the verandah skirting the front of the house. On the left to the garden, the stretches of the tea plantation added to the lushness. He could see what tea bushes with satin leaves were really like. Fragile trees interspersed between the bushes cast down puddles of shade. In the distance, he saw forested hills with a canopy of blue sky above them. The only sounds were the birds that had woken him and the clatter of dishes in the house. He went inside to wash and dress and suddenly realized that he was starving. As he emerged from his room, Vero appeared and pointed him to the wicker table in the verandah for a breakfast of fresh fruits, scrambled eggs and toast. He could not see Devika this morning. Just as he was finishing his tea, Sébastien heard the sound of a vehicle approaching. The gate was opened, a jeep swept up the driveway crunching on the gravel. A burly man with salt and pepper hair jumped out and came up the steps.

'Bonjour, bonjour! Sébastien!" They shook

hands. He recognized by his accent that the man was a *Mulâtre.* He spoke French with a strange drawl towards ending the vowels.

'How do you do? It's Paul- Paul Vince, very pleased to meet you. I hope you found everything to your satisfaction. Do you have everything you need? Are you liking our island?'

'Absolutely," said Sébastien. 'I had no idea what to expect, but it's been wonderful so far, everyone is really very kind and friendly, the place is beautiful, and sunshine every day!' The young man could go on and on, but this stranger was an explosion of good spirit and ready for a mission, as it seemed.

'Splendid," said Paul. "I'm relieved to hear that, to say the least! This place isn't everyone's cup of tea. Pardon the pun.'

Sébastien offered him breakfast.

'Thank you, no, I've already eaten. Wife takes

breakfast seriously you know, can't skip that, *sinon malheur*! Must get back to the factory. Madame Devika told me that you have not yet visited it, right? Splendid. Don't forget your hat. The sun of the tropics can be unforgiving, you know, although we are on the high plateau, it still can hit at midday.'

Sébastien got up, went to his room and rummaged for his hat. In a trail of dust, they set off in the jeep.

'Every tea plantation stretches for hundreds of acres, with a manager in charge, and one, maybe two assistants, the office staff, known as sirdar, and a large manual labour force, mostly women to pick and process the tea,' Paul shouted over the engine.

When they arrived at the factory, the first thing that struck the young man was the aroma of freshly cut tea. Paul explained that raw green leaf delivered from the plantation was laid out on racks on rolling tractor belts, ready to be fermented, rolled and dried. The manufacturing process transformed the leaf into coarse, black grain, rich and pungent, as it came off the drying belts. The island's excellent vanilla was added to some for local use. The islanders have got used to this flavour of tea and it's a must have on all occasions. The rest of the bulk of the tea would be boxed in plywood chests and shipped to auction houses in Calcutta and London. Sebastien was shown his office, a tiny room off a narrow corridor with a shiny red polished concrete floor.

In it was a desk piled with files, a wooden chair and an ancient filing cabinet. Everything was covered with a film of tea dust. A small window overlooked the Cana lily flower beds outside. The room was humble and basic, but the air was warm and fresh just as a warm Spring day in Finistère.

'I shall leave you to see some papers first, then, we can take a tour to the fields with the pickers. They start very early in the morning, as the delicate buds need picking without the sun scorching them. They normally finish by eleven o'clock, there must be some still there when we go.' Paul left whistling loudly a song of Brassens which Sébastien recognised immediately.

11 SHANTI

"No coincidence, no story," *Mawsi* recites, and that seems to settle everything, as it usually does, after she finishes telling us about the dream, she had last night. I don't know how many times my mother's sister has used this praising statement during the nineteen years I've been on this earth. I also feel as though I've heard versions of *Mawsi's* dream many times.

"A poor farmer carries freshly picked sousou to the market town to barter for rice and oil. He takes a misstep and tumbles down a cliff. This could have ended in a "terrible death" far from home—the worst thing that can happen to a coolie's descendent, but instead he lands in the camp of a wealthy salt seller. The salt

seller brews tea, the two men start talking, and ...

The coincidence could have been anything: the salt seller will now marry the farmer's daughter or the farmer's fall protects him from being washed away in a flood."

It was a good dream with no bad omens, which pleases everyone seated on the floor around the fire pit. As *Mawsi* said, every story, every dream, every waking minute of our lives is filled with one fateful coincidence after another. People and animals and leaves and fire and rain—we whirl around each other like handfuls of dried rice kernels being tossed up into the sky. A single kernel cannot change its direction. It cannot choose to fly to the right or to the left nor can it choose where it lands. Where they align fate, and nothing can change their destinies.

'Shanti, tell us a dream you had last night." "My dream?" The request surprises me, because neither of my late parents asked this of me before. I'm just a girl. Unimportant, as I've been told many times.

In our village, power and importance go in this order: the *sirdar*-headman; the *maraaz*, spirit priest—who keeps harmony between spirits and humans; and *Anney* the spiritual healer who has the ability to go into a trance, visit the tree God planted in the spirit world to represent each soul on earth, and then determine which incantations can be used to heal or enhance vitality. These men are followed next by all grandfathers, fathers, and males of any age. My mother was ranked first among women not only in our village but in the entire district. She was a *dai*, a midwife and so much more, treating men, women, and children as they pass through their lives. She was also known for her ability to interpret dreams. *Mawsi's* head covered with her *horni*, catching the firelight, as she waits for my response.

She always believed that I have inherited the gift of interpretation from my mother. The others bend their heads over their bowls slurping their bouillon and rice, nervous for me. I force myself to speak.

'I dreamed of a dog." Everyone is annoyed at this revelation.

'We allow dogs to live among us for three reasons,' *Mawsi* says reassuringly, trying to settle the family.

'They are essential for our lives, they alert us to bad omens, and they are kind to our children. What type of dog was yours?'

I hesitate once again. The dog in my dream stood on our corrugated tin roof, alert, his snout pointed upward, his tail wagging. Looking up at the sky and the stars. To me, he looked as though he was guarding our village, and seeing him made me feel confident that I would make it home safely.'

“Dogs are not humans, but they live in the human world. They are not of the spirit world neither, but they have the gift of seeing spirits. When you hear a dog howl or bark in the night, you know he has spotted a spirit and hopefully scared it away. Now answer me, girl,” she says, pushing her glass bracelets up her wrist, ‘what kind was yours?’

I know perfectly well that dreaming of a dog on the roof means that he hasn’t done his job and that a spirit has sneaked past the protection of the village’s spirit gate and is now roaming amongst us.

‘He frightened off an evil spirit.’ *Mawsi* was pleased, her eyes twinkling with the reflection of the dancing flames. She knew it. Her niece can be a plain looking girl, a tea picker, a labourer, but she has the gift.

Mawsi can’t see everything inside my head, as I always thought she could, or that I’ve got away with my fabrications. I feel pretty terrible until

I remind myself that I prevented my family from the worry my dream would have caused them. I lift my bowl to my lips and slurp down the last of my sousou bouillon. A few sweet mountain leaves slip into my mouth along with the fiery liquid. I had crushed a pickled piece of mango in it and used the arch of the stone to scoop out the bouillon. Chili flakes burn their way to my stomach. For as long as that heat lasts, I'll feel full.

When we leave the house, stars still shimmer above our heads. I carry a small basket on my back. My other family members have large baskets slung over their shoulders. Together we walk along the dirt lane that divides La Chartreuse village, which has about forty households and nestles in one of the many soft hills of the inner plateau of the island. Most of the homes are sheltered by old tea bushes. The tea terraces and gardens where we work, however, are outside the village. We join our neighbours, who live four houses away from us.

The youngest daughter, Mintah, is of my age. I could find my friend anywhere, because her cap is the most decorated of any girl in the field. Her delicate hands loved embroidering in her spare time, but she had to be a tea picker to help her family's finances. In addition to tea picking, her family grows pumpkins, cabbages and tomatoes which they sold at the Saturday market in the village square. They also cultivated turmeric, which they sell to *Anney*, the spirit priest to use in ceremonies, and also to villagers as a medicine. Many suffer from the agony of frequent sprains from walking barefoot on uneven terrain. Turmeric infusions also calmed the torment of the monthly cramps afflicting girls and women, or the mental anguish that comes from mothers nursing their babies with an unknown fever.

Mintah put a little money aside to buy coloured raffia strings, sequins, beads, ribbons and yarns when she could. They ended up on her cap decorated like a Christmas tree in the middle of the plainness of our own headgear. Apart from this difference, Mintah and I were like sisters, maybe closer than sisters, because we spend so much time side by side. As we continue toward our work, we leave the last house behind and proceed a little further until we reach the spirit gate. Carved figures of men with a huge curling moustache and long teeth are mounted on cut eucalyptus branches, as posts. On a slab of stone beneath them were offerings of coconut, cut lime, flowers, vermillion powder, candles, burnt camphor, and sometimes a glass of rum or some lit cigarettes. Be warned. If someone doesn't pass through the gate properly—touching it perhaps—then something terrible could happen, that's what we both have been warned by our families. So, each time we pass through the gate, we slow down, greet the altar with folded hands and bent heads, afterwards holding each other's hand tightly. Reassuring ourselves that we did not disturb the scene, we would run, air filling our lungs in big gulps, as if the devil was chasing us.

'Last night, *Mawsi* asked me again about my dream.' I told Mintah.

'There's nothing new with that one.' I didn't want to add to a topic so often spoken about, so I challenged her.

'Bet I can beat you to the top.' My feet knew this route well, and I hopped from rock to rock, jumping over exposed roots. In places, the dirt is powdery between my toes. In other spots, pebbles poke at the soft underparts of my arches. Since it's so damp, I sense more than seeing the old tea, camphor bark, and cassia trees, as well as stands of bamboo, towering around me.

I win again, which Mintah takes with a huge laugh.

'See you at the factory centre!'

I scramble up a steep stretch of mountain, my empty basket bouncing on my back then I skip ahead to catch up with my aunt. After some time, the pale night begins to fade, and the sky lightens with the first gleam of aurore.

Clouds catch tints of pink and lavender. Then everything brightens even more when the sun crests the mountain. It's the time of the day I like the most. The cicadas waken and begin to trill. My feet give way to a stretch of soft grass, fresh with dew. I enjoy walking on their cool dampness. Some people say that if you walk on dew you will grow tall. Some girls apply dew on their hair too, in the hope that their tresses will reach their knees. I walk on dew in the hope that I can reach beyond the horizon line one day, to meet my mother. This is where she has gone, *Mawsi* told me.

12 AT THE FACTORY

The men group together so they can have their own talk. I reached the tea terraces at last. I move slowly between the tightly packed rows of bushes, scanning the outermost branches for the bud and two, maybe three leaves that begin to unfurl as the sun's rays warm them. I gently nip the tiny cluster between my thumbnail and the side of my forefinger above the first joint. My thumbnail is stained dark green and the little pad of flesh, calloused. It's one I am proud of, a test mark of a good tea picker.

The *sirdar* makes his round after one hour. He bends, runs his hands through my leaves, fluffing and inspecting them.

'You're very good, girl, at finding the choicest

bud sets. Maybe too good." He glances in *Mawsi's* direction a few terraces away, then leans down and whispers, 'pick a little faster. And you can take some of the older and tougher leaves too. We need more leaves, not just ideal bud sets, from each bush.'

It's true, I have been concentrating in getting the youngest buds, whereas the tougher ones give more yield, hence more money. When my basket was full, I found Sooresh, who transferred my pickings into a burlap. We break for a lunch of rice, and vegetables, leftover from last night's dinner. Our aluminium *garde-manger* was wrapped into a napkin and tied well so there is no spill, when lunch included a curry or bouillon. It's also the time that the women take the opportunity to collect *'seet'*, a kind of cooperative potluck of money contributed each month. The sum total is given to one contributor, and the circle goes around until each one is paid their dividends. Women in villages have found this ingenious way to save money and multiply it into a good sum which helps them purchase goods they need in their house. A piece of furniture, a trousseau for a wedding, or for any special occasion where they would need some extra funds. A cooperative loan system enjoyed by the women only.

For some reason, the men preferred to spend any little extras they get at the local village Chinese boutique on cheap rum, beer and Eau-de-vie, eating fried *'cordonnier'* fish slices, sardines in oil, octopus *vindaye*, and *'Di pain maison'* as accompaniments. Eating and drinking seemed to be their main pastime.

We climb up and over more tea terraces, each one seemingly steeper than the last. Then we're back in the small forest, which has engulfed forsaken tea tree groves and gardens. Vines wrap around the trunks, which have become homes to orchids, and other plants. By the time we reach the tea collection centre, I'm so tired I want to cry.

Breakfast in the morning is a mug of tea, with a teaspoon of cooked rice in it, if there is any leftover.

We enter through the big gates of the factory into a courtyard. My vision flits around the open space, looking for Mintah's distinctive cap. Her family must have come and gone already. They might even be home by now, eating their lunch. My stomach calls to me, aggravated yet entranced by the smells coming from the food vendor stalls outside the gates. The flavour of skewered sweet potato on an open flame fills my senses. My mouth waters. An old woman sells from a cart inside the tea collection centre courtyard. The aroma is enticing, she brings piping hot curries with faratas. She makes garlic scallion and tamarind pickle which is so hot that it burns your tongue immediately. But despite this, it remains so popular that you need to queue for it, before it's even finished.

After lunch break, *Mawsi* and her friends take

our bags through a set of double doors that lead to the weighing area. On the other side of the courtyard, I spot a white man, his hair is glowing golden in the sun, his face pink and he has intense blue eyes. I have never seen him before. He suddenly turns around, as if he knew I was looking at him, and catches my gaze. I feel my cheeks burning, being caught looking at him. To my utter embarrassment, he moves towards me. I feel the ground giving way to my bare feet. I could be buried then and there, on the spot. For the first time, I feel conscious of my muddy calloused bare feet. I look down at them. Not a pretty sight. But that's how I am every day. Why should I feel different about them today?

"*Bonjour*, my name is Sébastien, I am the new R&D manager here, what is your name?" he asks.

'Shanti," I answered, my mouth happily stretched into a smile.

I raised my eyes to look at him, and I was lost in the most beautiful blue eyes I had ever seen from so close. They seemed like a puddle of the lagoon enclosed in each of them.

'I didn't think I was doing anything wrong.'

'Why do you think you did anything wrong?'

'Because the manager always asks one's name if one has made a mistake'

'No, you have not done anything wrong, I just wanted to ask how old you were, you seem quite young. Are your parents working here too?'

'Yes, *Missier*, everyone in the village works on the tea estate and factory. My *Mawsi* and *Mawsa* work here too'.

'What? *Mawsi* .... I don't understand'

'Ma Tante, Missier'

Shanti could not detach her eyes from those puddles of sea, Sébastien drew closer.

'So, are you of the right age to work?'

'Yes, I have worked here since I was fourteen'

'Hmmm... come into my office please, I want to check your file.'

I follow Sébastien in small steps. My teeth chatter, I shiver, and I want to pee. I want to run away, what will happen to me? Will he sack me?

I am thinking of my dream again, the one I made up and told *Mawsi* about. Was I being punished for it? Perhaps I should make an offering to *Dee* baba at the gates. An egg, no two eggs, maybe some cigarettes too. I will have to steal those from *Mawsa's* pocket. We make offerings to the mountains, rivers, dragons, heaven. We also make offerings every cycle to our ancestors. All of them involve food, so maybe an offering wasn't divided properly, or a dog grabbed some of it and ate it under the house. That's why I dreamt of the dog. Now this white man with blue eyes will punish me.

maybe spirits even look like him. White and spellbinding so that we mortals fall under their charm and are dragged to hell.

'Please take a seat, don't look so worried, am not going to hurt you'.

'So, you were going to hurt me?'

Peals of new sweat were now dripping from my neck and trickling down my chest, I was so scared. The man looked at me following the sweat drops to where they disappeared. He seemed a bit troubled for a second.

Sébastien did not like seeing such young girls working on the tea plantation. Starting at fourteen, that was sheer child labour. Why was she not in school? He found her card and located her file. So, she was nineteen, not underage. He felt relieved.

'You may go now, and ... don't you wear any slippers?'

I glanced at my feet and felt embarrassed once

again.

'Non *Missier*, they slip in the mud, and I can fall. It's better to walk barefoot to get a good grip down the slopes.'

Sébastien couldn't believe how such a pretty girl could be picking tea and walking barefoot.

This island is surely opening new realities to him. His heart is swaying towards Devika, but she is very private, and does not allow him to be close to her so he could advance his way to her. Now, this beauty in front of him. His male side was blatantly somersaulting with confusion. He wanted to protect this young girl. He looked at her slender sun-tanned arms, lips so tender, almond shaped deep brown eyes, and hair shining and bouncing back the least ray of light. He looked again at her, while she drew small steps to retreat from the room. Her body was backlit sending a slim silhouette. She looked so fragile and innocent. He looked through the window when Shanti reached outside. She turned around and stared at him for a moment. And left.

A couple of hours later, *Mawsi* ladles the salt fish *rougaille* and dhal onto our plates, followed by sounds of slurping, and chewing. These are among the happiest I've heard in my life. As I gnaw from a fish bone, little sparks of images fly through my head. I recollect Sébastien and his deep blue eyes. In my dream last night, an omen of seeing a dog on the roof told me I was going to get into trouble. A sweet trouble, that's what I was heading towards. One which was inevitable. After all, I may have inherited my mother's gift of dream interpretation. At that moment, I missed her a lot. I wished she was still alive; I would have confided in her. My mixed emotions, my heart fluttering. When would I see him again? *Mawsi* was right.

No coincidence, no story.

13 FIRE WALKING

The omens are particularly worrisome. It's the season of spirits. It's raining. Even the dogs have stopped barking.

For the next ten days, our village follows ceremonial abstinence. It's the period of the fire walking ceremony. A feast each evening at the temple, with offerings, devotional songs, mantras, and women clad in their colourful sarees. No meat, no fish, no egg, no brinjals, no bitter gourds, no onions, no garlic. Everyone is busy cooking extra each evening to make up for the banned foods.

The day had arrived, Mariamman was decked in her finest and taken for a ceremonial around the village. The procession stopped at most road crossings whence devotees came forward with offerings of coconut, flowers, fruits and incense sticks. Back at the temple, the fire had been blazing all night in the pit. I stood at a distance from the long bed of heated embers, neatly levelled to receive its guests, rubbing my hands together for warmth.

Any closer and the heat would have been uncomfortable. A crowd of workers stood around it too, some squatting in groups looking away from the flare, while others sauntered around, shielding their eyes from it with their hands. Those tending the fire were clearly wilting in the heat. They had been storing large quantities of firewood, burning it down all night to the cinders that had now been arranged into an ordered bed about 12m long, 1m wide and 30cm deep. Another group was pouring buckets of water on the red-hot ground around. Steam spewed as water met scorched earth and cooled it. The temple priest rang a large bronze bell in his hand and made offerings of rice, bananas, and coconut. He walked around the bed, sprinkling holy water to sanctify it, stopping at intervals to pick up and drop handfuls of burning coals with his bare hands, as easily as if they were marbles. People in the watching crowd whispered to each other and nodded in awed approval: surely this superhuman feat was an indication that the gods were on his side!

The firewalkers were ready. They had spent the last ten days preparing themselves, fasting and praying in a state of purity. Each day, after completing their work on the estate, they had met at the temple and chanted prayers together under the direction of the priest. Frugal meals were brought from their homes to the temple, where they ate together. At night, they slept on its veranda, a strongly bonded team whose closeness shielded them from temptation towards any immoral activity. Having spent the previous night cloistered inside the temple, prevented from falling asleep by continuously chanting prayers, they were now immersed in the final ritual cleansing in the river below. As each one pulled himself out of the river, his forehead was anointed with *bhasmam* – ceremonial ash and vermilion, as well as a garland of jasmine and marigold flowers which was placed around his neck. Some smeared themselves all over with the ash. Together they climbed up the riverbank to the temple to the increasing tempo of the high-pitched kettle drums traditionally used in temples in this area, some grimacing, others wearing vacant grins, seemingly in hypnotic trances, and trooped towards the bed of burning coals. As they stepped onto it, loud cheers rose from the crowd. While some ran across, taking just a few long strides, others ambled, ankle-deep in burning coals. The firewalkers have committed themselves to the sanctifying ritual as penance to the gods. They come from families who have faced a hardship, perhaps a marriage which has not yet resulted in children, or a financial crisis, or disease or the untimely death of a family member. They have been nominated by the head of the family to take part as an offering to *Mariamman*, the demanding deity. Occasionally a young person decides to take part of their own volition. The people of La Chartreuse, in comparison with other villages, were rustic folks accustomed to lives of deprivation and hard labour. They could not claim prosperity or culture; their capital was their endurance and physical strength. They had left their homes but carried their gods with them since they came as indentured workers. Their faith and devotion had nurtured them through difficult times, despair, and disease. And the high-risk fire walking was not just a culmination of their faith but a demonstration of their prowess, a fulcrum of prestige.

Over the years, no matter how many times I viewed the fire walking ceremony, it never lost its impact as a morning of mysticism, devotion, and awe; a tremendous superhuman feat. Loga, the son of the priest told me repeatedly about the powers of *Mariamman*, the temple deity evoked in this ritual, its purity, and the miracles he had seen. I was fascinated. He said that *Mariamman* spreads the *pallu* of her saree over the embers for her devotees when they walk so, they feel no pain. That was a grace to anyone who has adhered to their fast well, with utmost devotion.

Once it's full cycle of ceremonial abstinence ends, after the main event, life seems to return to normal. The women go back to embroidering, sewing, and doing chores besides their daily tea picking. The men go back to smoking, drinking at the Chinese tavern, playing Dam on the floor and trading stories. For me, I continued longing for the day I will see *Missier* again.

Mawsi received the invitation for the *Dee* puja - *gardien la cour*, on Sunday. She was actively into preparations as of Wednesday for *Mawsa* to get to town to purchase some ingredients for the ceremony. It is customary to do this ritual each year, sometimes twice, if the situation is not good in the village. *Dee Baba* is the village spirit. The protector of the community.

'Humans and spirits, cows and wild boars, chickens and birds of prey needed to be separated,' I was told repeatedly.

'Separated. Exactly,' *Mawsi* says.

"Since the decision to divide the universe happened during the day, men were first to pick in which realm they wanted to live. They chose the earth with its trees, mountains, fruits, and game. Spirits were given the sky, leaving them angry forever after. To this moment, they have retaliated by causing problems for humankind."

I've heard this story many times but knowing that she's telling it on my behalf makes my heart hurt. "*In the wet season,*' she goes on, *'spirits descend to earth with the rain, bringing with them disease and floods. In spring, as the dry season begins, noise is made to encourage malevolent spirits to move on. That's why bells are kept ringing during the ceremony."*

I had no interest in such stories. For me, killing an animal to feed an invisible spirit, without any guarantee it truly was fed off the blood, made my skin crawl with disgust and anger. It was pure murder. I retreat into a corner and come by only when called by an insistent *Mawsi*, who seems to need me more during such occasions. She reckoned that because I may have the 'gift' that I am entitled to witness all these nonsense rituals.

So, on the day, people came to gather around the spirits gate. Fruits, flowers were offered, coconuts broken in half, incense ignited, camphor burned, cigarettes lit as kids watched in amazement. They believed that *Dee Baba* was smoking as the ash gathered, half a loaf of bread laid on a piece of banana leaf, and a tin of sardines, top curled open. A spoon with a camphor piece was lit and swirled over the head of a black rooster, before its head was chopped off. Afterwards, the poor animal was feathered, gutted and cooked into a spicy curry and fed to anyone who fancied a titbit.

The priest said it was a blessed morsel of '*cari coq*' as *Dee Baba* was pleased with the sacrifice. He would ensure that the crop was kept bountiful, the workers protected from any mishap, children and unmarried girls shielded from bad spirits. That included me. Many avoided eating the curry as it was believed that whoever ate the curry, offered to the spirits, had to do the extensive offerings each year. And nobody wanted to incur those extra expenses.

*

The sound of knocking awakens me the next morning. After being up in the small hours the previous days for preparations, each one of us had at long last collapsed and fallen into a deep sleep.

A magnificent dawn began to suffuse the sky beyond the hills. Our favourite rooster started its loud cock-o-doodling as if its life depended on it. I tried counting how many times it did it, but sometimes it felt it would never stop. My chores started after the rooster stopped. I was to make the morning tea for the family. Usually, the shiny brass Primus stove made it seem to go quicker, by its vigorous blue flame, but the process was the same every day.

In most homes, the first tea of the morning was sacred. It was not infused in a teapot like when served to guests, but boiled in a *dekchi* with milk, cardamom and smashed fresh ginger root until it became a dark muddy colour. The process was the same each day. I boil some water in the large *deckchi*, add the spices then spoon in the leaves from the tin caddy on the counter and let them steep.

My movements are quick and deft with the efficiency born of habit. A proper pot of tea, just the way *Mawsi*, had taught me, with some nice golden sugar to sweeten, completes the brew.

The first cup always lands for me.

By the time the whole household is awake and makes their appearance one by one in the kitchen for their hot cuppa, I would already be with my second.

The bread seller arrives early on his bicycle to do his round of hawking loaves to each house. But in our household, the *'dipain maison'* was considered an extra luxury. So, it was not present daily on the table for a frugal breakfast. Instead, some faratas were made and eaten with leftover curry. The tea we drink is also part of the thriftiness that *Mawsi* used to manage the finances.

Mawsa buys off the discarded dust of tea from those packed for exports. Almost everyone does so, as the tea is fresher, of better quality, and cheaper too. La Chartreuse in fact could be called a tea village. Everyone works in the same tea estate and factory and drinks the same tea. Our lives depend upon Bonne Espérance, and how well it fares. We have plenty of sugar and tea, hence our lives were punctuated by generous amounts of both, twice a day.

14 GRAND BAZAARS

Work on the tea plantation is mainly gendered: women are "considered" to be efficient pluckers and men did most of the maintenance work in the factory. Often, despite the gendered division of labour, men and children also engaged in the work of tea-plucking, along with other kinds of work. They were fortunate to be involved in the manufacture of tea, because everything in that industry depends upon good timing and good teamwork, and strictly understood hierarchies of responsibility.

Shanti loved the huge and beautiful machinery

in the factory and could not resist rolling up her sleeves and joining with the men helping the mechanics or engineer when it broke down. Machinery was so much easier to deal with than people. There was always a precise set of reasons why a machine may not be working, and there were always completely logical solutions. People were slippery and elusive, changeable and moody. You thought you understood them and then found out that you did not. You thought they loved you, and then they suddenly turned spiteful or indifferent. If she was not a girl, she would have been happier working with the machines, rather than picking tea.

Going to work today meant she could see Sébastien again. This hope kept Shanti keen to reach the fields with a lighter foot for a week. Over the past couple of days, she had found sleep increasingly fitful and was often awake in the small hours, battling strange, disconcertingly deep thoughts about the random nature of choice, fate and destiny; thoughts that made no sense at all in the cold light of day. Although she could never recall the details of waking, she was visited by a recurring dream; one that left a lingering memory of a pair of tender blue eyes and a feeling of a hand having touched her heart.

Saturday came with a dent, a day when she went with *Mawsi* to grand bazar. Not a chance to see Sébastien. They went early in the morning, exploring the streets of Port Louis, before it became too hot to venture out. Even in the cooler part of the day, it was stifling, and Shanti failed to understand how much the humidity affected her body. She had got acclimatized to the coolness of the high plateau too much.

The capital city with its crowded cobbled streets, colourful fruits and spices exuded exotic smells. It was impossible not to be intoxicated by the sweet fragrance of hibiscus, frangipani, dried octopus, vanilla and ylang-

ylang, the whiff of salt from the sea mingling with the smell of fish, the heady scent of incense which caught the back of her throat.

As she walked past the imposing white mosque, the Jama Masjid, she saw men entering the cool shady courtyard ready for their ablutions before reading their prayers. The aroma of buttery naan and cardamom reached her nostrils from a nearby open glass caddy. A middle aged rotund Muslim woman with a head scarf was selling them, wrapping one swiftly in a paper bag. The unspeakably hustle and bustle of street sellers, textile and hardware shops, stationary alley ways made an incongruous mix of trades on one single road. The smell of food cooking pervading the air, as meat was stirred into smoking oil or mingled with sesame and soy by the Chinese street hawkers. She marvelled at how the cooks were able to stand beside steaming vats of noodles and dumplings, fish ball soups, rapidly stirring the food in their wok, in this oppressive heat.

Arsenal street at the junction of the Royal road displayed some of the most prolific dim sums and street Chinese foods. The lines of basic benches at the stalls were never empty, people would prefer to stand and eat rather than miss a bowl while searching for a place to sit.

Shanti loved coming to the city and taking with her all these images, and smells to last until she is back again. But today, her heart and mind felt far from the crowd. They just sounded like a big hum to her ears, people passing by, like she was alone, and nothing made much sense to her. Sébastien had truly taken over her mind. She could not wait for yet another day before she could see him. It had to be soon. In the matters of the heart, even the discernible eyes of *Mawsi* could not guess what turmoil was going on in Shanti's heart.

They got into the dusty market where traders had set up stalls and laid out their wares. Trays of fresh vegetables lay next to each other, some on trestle tables, their bright colours of red, green, yellow and white, competing for attention: long white daikons, mounds of pointed red chilies, bunches of *vouëm* - long green beans, and canary yellow *pâtissons*.

At the far corner of the open square stood the fish section. Fish of all shapes, sizes and hues lay inert on slabs of ice. Capitaine, Dame Bery, Cato, Mullet, Mackerel, Tuna, Rouget, Tazar and Cordonnier, once swimming happily in the ocean, now laid out on the slab, waiting to be picked by a keen buyer. Next to them, an old woman bustled around cages of live crabs. Shanti was not keen on the fish smell, so she left her aunt bargaining for some Capitaine, and came out to take in some fresh air. The moment *Mawsi* emerged from the smelly fish market, Shanti went ahead. She made it to the *Alouda* shop. It was a plain wooden shack, where two men shouted loudly "*alouda frappé, alouda glacé*" it was a magic of a place. Most of the shoppers stopped by to quench their thirst with tall glasses of rose flavoured milk with basil seeds and grated grass jelly with lots of ice. Some even asked for the ultimate luxury of two scoops of vanilla ice cream in it. This was their must-have each time they came to Port Louis. They both had their glasses of *alouda* and swallowed them down slowly to avoid brain freeze. Next to the shop, was a stall which had been there ever since Shanti remembered. It was held by a Chinese lady. Jars of sweets, prawn crackers, pickled ginger, and sweet and sour dried plums filled the shelves. To the front stood a wooden trestle. In one section of this long counter lay banana-leaved parcels of rice cooked in coconut cream with freshly grated coconut. But, best of all, at the far end, stood an ice crusher which churned out balls of grated ice. An array of flavoured multicoloured syrups stood in glass bottles. The shaved ice was served in cups doused generously with the fruit syrups. If she had not had the *alouda*, this would be what Shanti would go for, as the perfect thirst quencher. An oasis in this hot, humid mad crowd. Bamboo and rattan baskets, some filled with dried fish and others with splayed dried octopus from Rodrigues, were lined in neat rows on either side of the dry goods market. They always buy their ration of dried fish from a toothless seller as dark as the night. He was a kind fellow who always weighed some grams more for *Mawsi*, for being such a long-time regular customer. Next, some medicinal herbs were purchased from Mr Armoogum, the herbalist. *Mawsa* needed some detox herbs to apparently cleanse his kidneys. I thought it would be a good idea for him to stop drinking. That would save some money, and *Maws*i could splurge on some more goat meat for us all.

15 FIRST FLUSH

The first weeks of April. It is still cool in the early morning hours. The clouds in the east are tinged with pink, orange, and purple. The sun has managed to raise only the tip of its upper rim above the horizon, and the moon, having already lost her lustre, is now only a pale, yellowish ghost in the sky. The morning star is still twinkling in the east over a range of hills. The people of Bonne Espérance tea estate stirred from sleep, about an hour ago.

The tea pickers had gathered in the open area in front of the tool shed, where two men dressed in thick shorts, light cotton shirts, and wide-brimmed hats, stood poised to allot the labourers their work for the day. The sound of house sparrows chirping loudly on the neighbouring banyan and tamarind trees announced that the day might be a good one.

A group of women, heard before they are seen, are moving gracefully through the morning mist, saree clad, each with a light jumper and a scarf tied around their head. From the direction of their living quarters, their voices drift towards the open meeting place in front of the tool shed. The colours of their saris and skirts encompass the entire range of the rainbow. The sirdar, or overseer, stands in front of them, under the light bulb fixed above the door of the tool shed, reads from a list on the clipboard he clutches in his hand. The women join different groups when their names are called out and assignments given. Each group moves away to the part of the garden where they will work through the day, their bangles tinkling melodiously like wind chimes.

This is the first pick of the year, the first flush. The equivalent Beaujolais nouveau for tea.

There have been droughts and cyclones, all knocking at the delicate bush buds. All through the winter, the bushes have been dormant, but they are now lively, lush green. There is much excitement among the women, who know precisely which leaves to pick and which ones to discard. The ones that have opened up make their way into their baskets, while the twisted or overgrown ones are tossed out, and unopened ones reserved for picking later. Each picker hopes to make a little more money and the ambition has them overstretching themselves to pick more than the required quantity. Spring, so called here in the tropics is more of an allegory, is the season of hope, debts will be repaid and that this year will bring a good harvest. Sébastien has decided to accompany the sirdar today and see the rounds of inspections through the main fields. He used his jeep to cover most of the tracks but walked through the dense green bushes to meet up with some of the pickers. The women greet him with smiles everywhere he goes, some with a little giggle, like adolescents.

'Good morning Shanti!' Sébastien had spotted the young girl next to the row where a multi-coloured cap with scintillating sequins had caught his eye as well as those of the morning's sun. It was Mintah. Where Mintah was, Shanti could not be far. The young woman froze upon hearing the young man calling her name. She almost needed to pinch herself to believe it was true. Finding her in the vast fields among the pickers was nothing less than finding a needle in a haystack. But he found her! So, he must have been looking for her.

"What is your aunt like?" he asked suddenly. He wanted to have some idea of the woman whose permission he would need to seek if he were to court the girl. His eyes took in everything from her hair to her knee-length cotton wrapper beneath which the skirt hung down to her ankles. Her feet were bare, just like the first time he saw her; her untidy hair was divided into two braids. There seemed to be no artifice about this woman.

She touched her warm cheeks with her cool fingers. There was no reason to say about being mismatched. Why was she not embarrassed anymore, to be seen dressed this way? Hair is tousled, and still barefoot, dressed in the plainest dress! Yet it all felt so natural, like this is the way it was meant to be.

‘Such men surely are used to different types of women. Not like me’ thought Shanti. ‘But there he was looking at me, smiling while his deep blue eyes squinted to avert the sun’s gaze’.

‘*Bonjour Missier*, how are you?

My *Mawsi* is a nice person. Why do you ask?’ Shanti could only mutter these words which sounded idiotic, but could she even think straight and say some intelligent and witty words? No. Her heart right now was beating so fast, she could hear it inside her ears. She felt a little dizzy too. Why did she lose her countenance each time she saw this man?

There was a distant sound of women's voices, singing as they worked. Shanti could not see them from where she stood, but she recognized the rhythm of a work song. A strange, undeniable conviction came over her. She can do this. Sébastien felt closer than she imagined. She had seen a girl praying at the small temple of Hanuman, the monkey God, where she went to pray too. Was it a sign?

A call from Devi in the shape of the girl, to give her acknowledgement that Shanti should persevere with her feelings for the man with golden hair. She had smeared Bhagwan Ganesha, the elephant god idol with orange coloured sindoor, and lit a small terracotta lamp to implore his wisdom to help guide her.

'Tell me Shanti, is picking tea what you really like doing?'

'Everyone picks tea *Missier* Sébastien, what else would I do?'

'I thought you might like a job where you are

more sheltered, and not have to walk barefoot'

Hearing this, Shanti felt her cheeks going red. Without letting her say a word, he continued.

'Maybe you can work at the villa, for Mrs Devika. Can you do house chores, like ironing and cooking you know ... those sorts of things?'

Shanti was surprised by this sudden offer. She was also a bit disappointed. She thought he had come to look for her. Her heart made a leap. She could not utter a word.

'I spoke to Mrs Devika about you, and she certainly would welcome an extra pair of hands for Veronique. She is the house help and also the nanny to the baby.'

'Madame has a baby?'

'Yes, a girl ... so will you consider it? Talk to your Aunt and let me know. If you are OK with it, you may start straight away.'

'Thank you *Missier*. And where is the villa?'

'I will come and pick you up, if you send me a word through Sooresh, you know him, he works at the factory.'

'Yes, he is a close friend of my *Mawsa*, I will let you know through him. *Missier* ... May I ask why you are offering me to work at the villa? Is my tea picking not good?'

Sébastien gave her a wide smile, 'it's just that I believe you deserve better than working under this harsh sun. Besides I can see you more often and won't have to look for your friend Mintah's cap to find you. Goodbye, and see you very soon.'

'Yes ... goodbye' the words died in Shanti's throat as Sébastien returned to the jeep and drove in a *pétarade* of the wheels.

Shanti was thinking, 'so he did come looking for me'. That was enough to quieten the mad thumping of her heart. .... besides I can see you more often' he had said. Lord Hanuman answered her prayers fast. She has to return to him to offer some sugar *ladoos* as thanks.

Back home, Shanti replayed her meeting with Sébastien a hundred times in her head, halting on the precise words he had said to her and analysing them to understand their true meaning. With her elegant oval face, golden olive complexion, long dark hair, and intense brown eyes, Shanti was a true beauty. Yet, she wasn't aware of it. Nobody had said before that she was beautiful. Her body language mirrored the sadness she carried inside. Where most young women of her age moved with effortless grace, hers were contained. Where amusement and joy should have lit her face, there was melancholy. Although *Mawsi* and *Mawsa* looked after her properly, she could not forget that she was an orphan, and she never stopped working to prove her mettle, grateful that they had taken her in. If it's not chores, it's picking tea. She gave all her earnings to *Mawsi* and had never asked for money. She was content to have a roof over her head, a bed to sleep, a hot meal each day, just grateful to belong to a family.

That evening, Shanti made a delicious chicken curry with new potatoes she had dug from the garden. She also rolled and made heaps of her famous spiralled flaky *faratas*, bread and butter pudding which she baked in a Bain Marie till it was golden and smelling delicious. Everyone was delighted at the lip-smacking meal and *Mawsa* asked if it was someone's birthday.

No, Shanti was just very happy, and she already was feeling in the skin of being a help at the villa. She would cook delicious things to serve Sébastien. She told *Mawsi* about Sebastien's offer. The latter was quick to say yes.

Working for the Mistress of Bonne Espérance was nothing short of having a huge promotion. What pride she would have telling her friends that her niece worked at the villa of Madame.

The future for Shanti was looking very rosy.

The next morning, she saw two rainbows and took to it that the heavens were being clement to her. She was thankful to God but missed her mother very much. She wished she was alive to share her joy with her.

16 THE VILLA

Shanti was brought to the villa by Sébastien as promised. She took her steps on the paved black basaltic porch to the terracotta tiled verandah leading to the beautifully polished hardwood flooring of the hallway. The young woman was warmly welcomed by Devika and Veronique, both showed her around the house, with a short introduction to what was expected, as part of her duties.

That day, Devika was trying out different tea brews, trying to select which ones were strong or mellow in their taste. She needed a tea taster to validate her tastings. She had some great ideas which she was eager to discuss with

Sébastien. Lately he had been coming home late and leaving early in the morning.

The arrival of Shanti proved a good thing indeed. The baby seemed happy with her during the day, and she helped Veronique with the best of her endeavours. Sébastien was content with placing the young girl at the villa. Some days, one feels that some good and it was enough to feel content about it.

*

People may think that a tea taster's job was only to taste the quality of tea produced on the estate. He gets the highest pay among the manual workers, other than the sirdar. It may seem to be an outstanding career option but as a tea taster, one only needs to taste different types of tea and find what makes them distinctive.

On the job, the tea taster needs to visit other plantations, researching and learning about what other varieties were around. This helps restaurants, hotels and companies provide their customers with the best quality tea. A tea taster has a strong knowledge of preparation, processing, minute details and history of the tea. There is a high importance of decision making in this career. A tea taster has the understanding of quality and how to discriminate between main notes. Communication skill is also vital, as well as awareness of the tea market and the emerging trends and forces. Tasting hundreds of cups of tea may seem to be stupid for a commoner, especially when you need to pick the best value out of hundreds. While having a sharp enough memory to recall the details of taste and preparation for each brew, the tea taster decides if the crop has yielded to quality tea or not. The future of a tea estate depended on a good tea taster.

Devika needed to find one such person.

17 RISHI

The majority of the workers of Bonne Espérance were Hindus and followed the praying system as other neighbouring villages. In La Chartreuse, different idols under different names were worshiped. If they saw an old tree, a stone was constructed under the tree, and workers started venerating it as a god. In the course of time, the workers pooled money and built temples for goddess *Mariamman* and Lord Ganesh. Festivals came and went, celebrated to overcome problems in their lives.

Many were surprising singers besides being tea pickers, and played an important part in the celebrations, by singing devotional songs. However, when it came to tea tasting, it was sometimes frowned upon because of the caste system. As having a nose and a tongue which can discern subtle tastes and flavours is a rare thing. If by accident, this person happens to be of the lower caste of the *chamars*, then the rest of the people might not want to have anything to do with him. Even though the tea tasting would not have impacted on the bulk. Such was the prejudiced thinking of people who had still not parted with their country of their forefathers. It was a rare thing, but it did happen.

Fortunately, Devika was not someone who gave way to such beliefs nor tolerated it on her estate. *Chaman*, *Doossad*, *Kohri*, or *Babuji*, for her, everyone had their place under the sun.

The Tea Plantation workers' primary task was to cultivate tea plants, maintain the fields, pluck green leaves, support the factory, cultivate ancillary plants, maintain buildings, and complete the process of manufacture of tea ready for consumption. The road system had to be well maintained to provide easy access to the various fields, and transport of green leaf to the factory. All workers were supplied with housing according to their job category and status, along with some plots of land for their vegetable cultivation or animal husbandry.

A female worker's task was to pluck tea leaves, therefore, called a plucker by profession. Also, every labourer formed the backbone of the tea estate. They lived, worked and died on the tea plantation where they were born, virtually making even their remains become manure for the tea bushes.

Plucking tea leaves is a very skilled operation and is traditionally the work of a woman. They have acquired this skill of selecting the 'two leaves and a bud' over the years. No machine can match their uniquely nimble fingers which break the tender leaves and transfer them in handfuls to the baskets they carry on their backs. The speed at which they carry out this task is just astonishing. In the recent past, *gooni* bags had replaced baskets made of cane or bamboo.

Urged on by the chill of the short winter days, the tea plants were now forming their third flush of tender shiny leaves, lending a tantalizing fragrance to the crisp highland air. The tea pickers had been at work assiduously trying to make the best of the season. Large bins were drying the picked leaves and the smoking process of turning them dark, had begun.

Sébastien worked relentlessly, aiming to achieve a good yield to send to London. He was sure that this year's crop would be of good quality. Devika had asked him to have a chat with her as soon as he could.

The young woman, besides her baby and Bonne Espérance had nothing more in store, to guide and lead her life. She had not heard from her husband. She had always assumed that she would grow up to be a *pativrata* and remain devoted to her for the rest of her life. Having been reared on stories of powerful goddesses that were Sita, Savitri, and Shakuntala, examples of devoted Hindu wives, she found it hard to believe that now, at age twenty-four, she was alone.

For now, she needed to find a taster who could tell whether her experimental decoctions could be viable for exploitation. She visited some people in the village, recommended by either Veronique or Marcel, but those acquaintances did not meet the level of a potential taster. How about going directly to the pickers? They will have better insight in a plant they toil with day and night.

When Devika set off on one of her frequent visits to the plantation, she could not have anticipated that an unexpected encounter was going to answer all her expectations. As she picked her way along a narrow trail, winding across the side of a precipitous La Chartreuse foothill carpeted with shiny deep green tea bushes, she heard the tinkle of prayer bells that someone was ringing in the distance. It was probably *Anney*, the priest.

She stopped and looked proudly at the hundreds of acres under the plantation she now owned. It was a piece of heaven. When she reached the tea-processing factory, a long two-story building set into the hillside; a tall man emerged from the office. He had slick oiled hair parted neatly on the side, wore a brown linen shirt and a pair of khaki trousers. The sun lit his face on the side, revealing his sharp nose and deep-set eyes. He must have noticed her, for he halted and pressed his hands together at chest level, in a greeting.

'Namaste Madam, good to see you here, we have not formally met, but I know who you are. My name is Rishi Deonand.'

'*Pranaam* Rishi, I am Devika'

'Oh Madame, you spoke in *shudh* Sanskrit. It's the language of the gods. How do you know it? Have you learned Sanskrit?'

'No Rishi, sadly at this point, I'd rather be an ordinary mortal for whom a good cup of tea is the best bonus of the day. It's a difficult language. I just say it the same way I have learnt saying it from my *Nani.*'

'For me, I learnt a bit in the afternoon classes at the *baitka*, as my father wanted me to continue the generation of priests we come from, but I was not keen to do so. However, I like the language, it has so much depth to it. If we were speaking Sanskrit, I'd have said the soft lavender sari you're wearing is a swath of the sky'.

'Oh, that's beautifully put. So, what exactly do you do here Rishi?'

'I am a tea taster, Madam'.

Devika could not believe what she just heard.

Rishi pointed out a load of boxed tea for shipment to an auction house in London. He had blended and tasted an assortment of teas from the factory. The first blends need to be tested and tasted.

'So, you are the Taster of Bonne Espérance!'

'Yes, I am indeed .... your humble servant, I have been doing this job for the last 5 years.' His face glowed as he explained how the vanilla note of the last mélange was still lingering in his mouth, and how much the work meant to him.

'No chilies, no onions in my food, and I don't ever touch alcohol or tobacco. Nothing that would dull my palate.'

Although gifted, Rishi had been taught tea tasting at an early age. He could still recite the procedure: "Slurp the tea to aerate it, roll it on your palate, gurgle, consider, and spit." The taste buds and olfactory system of the body would register the taste instantly.

Before she inherited the estate, Devika was happy to simply boil the water, throw in some tea leaves, let it brew and add a touch of milk. She drank her daily cup without much thought to it. But now, it means a whole new universe of knowledge one needs to acquire to run a business. Even so, she was aware that the tea bushes belonged to various pedigrees, and to assess the quality of the manufactured tea, a taster was needed with a keen nose, sharp taste buds, and discerning eyes, as well as knowledge of the market. Rishi must be a rare individual who possessed all these qualities. Looks like Devika had just hit the jackpot. She pressed to invite the man to the villa to discuss her latest ideas.

'Why don't you come over for dinner on Sunday? I would like to share some experiments with you and seek your opinion.'

'Dinner? I would be honoured to gladly accept Madam.'

'Right then, let's say 6 o'clock? Veronique serves dinner at 7 p.m., so we shall have an hour to talk. Of course, I shall tell her about the chilies, onions and garlic.'

'Namaste Madam see you on Sunday, next'.

Devika came home with ideas stumbling in her head, she was too eager to see Veronique and Shanti to tell them about Rishi. Veronique greeted her with a chilled drink of bergamot. It was refreshing after going out in the sun.

"Veronique, Ah! That's so delicious, thank you. I met someone at the factory, his name is Rishi and he is a tea taster. He is just the person I was looking for, and all this time he was working at the factory. I had no idea. I invited him over on Sunday for dinner. He does not eat chilies, onions, or garlic.'

She fumbled with her sari border. 'He's a rather interesting fellow, seems to know a lot about tea, and ...' Shanti stopped short of cutting aubergine, she had a vague look on her face.

'Shanti, Is everything alright?'

'Yes Madam, thank you, everything is alright, I couldn't stop myself overhearing your conversation, allow me to tell you a little about Rishi, some things he may not have mentioned.'

'Oh really? Is there anything that I should know?'

'He comes from a Brahmin high caste family; his father works as a clerk at some trading company in Port Louis besides being a *pandit*. They live in the older part of the town near the reservoir. For all that, he has a good education, for his parents somehow managed to send him to college. The fellow is a born tea taster. We have a saying in the industry that 'when it comes to tea tasting, you are as good as your palate' and he has a brilliant one. He is very dedicated and disciplined. He wanted to be a field supervisor, however, his unique skills turned him into a tea taster.'

'Thank you, Shanti, but how do you know so much about him and why the worry on your face, if he has such good qualities?'

'Because my *Mawsi* knows his mother, they have been friends since in school, and she wanted me to marry him'

'That's really a good thing, If I understand. He looks like a fine man and will make a good husband.'

'I have refused ...three times.'

'Oh! Surely, you have your own reason for doing that. But I will find out more when he comes over on Sunday.'

Shanti suddenly felt cold air surrounding her. The prospect of having two suitors in the same room was daunting. Not that Sébastien had declared his feelings to her but in her heart and mind, he had already done so when he offered her to work at the villa. He said, *'to be close to him'*. That sealed anything unsaid.

Could Rishi see through her when he comes for dinner? That would be most inconvenient for everyone. She would certainly not want news reaching her home about her love affair with a white man. She needed to do something about it, before disaster hit her love life. The saddest part was that it had not yet begun.

Late afternoon on the following day, Shanti found herself in front of a tea worker's residence, situated on a dirt road on the edge of the tea plantation. She pretended she needed some personal belongings from home, and Veronique asked her to go when all the chores were completed. Beti was in her cot for her afternoon nap, when Shanti left the villa.

She had mustered her courage to tell this small lie. Now being in front of this house, her heart was pounding. A long-time family servant whose brother worked in the tea factory had disclosed to her the details of a secret spiritual healer and had guided her to this location. She decided to pay a visit.

18 A SPIRITUALIST

The one-story breeze block house displayed a tin roof, painted sky blue. A tangled thicket of coffee fenced the front, a small shrine for Hanuman, Mahavir Swami painted in white had its orange prayer flags mounted on three bamboo poles, fluttering in the gentle breeze. Near the entrance were three flowerpots, where waves of tall yellow and red hibiscus flowers grew. With the afternoon sun looming above, the landscape was immobile, almost expectant. From somewhere, a hen clucked and made its appearance followed by some chicks. Shanti was growing anxious with a feeling of unease. She took a glance through a wide-open window where the curtains were knotted to allow air to come in. A tall man with a faint frown greeted her.

'Namaste, what can I do for you?'

'Namaste, I have some matters to address, and have come for your help. Dhiraj at the tea factory, sent me to you saying you are a spiritual healer.'

'Indeed, you have come to the right house, please come in.'

Inside was a minimalist room with just a table with a Formica top and some chairs, a vase of fresh cut flowers stood on the side, while an array of deities in framed photos were hung on the wall. A small chest laid next to where he took his seat. A Bengali sang, breaking the silence between them. The air inside the room smelled fragrant of camphor, incense and spices.

'You see, I have someone who wants to marry me, but I refused. Now, I work at the villa, and this person is visiting on Sunday.'

'So, where is the problem?'

'I don't want him to know that I like *Missier* Sébastien ...'

'Who is that?'

'He lives there, he is French and is a very good person, he likes me too.'

'Do you mean you like him?'

'Yes, euh ...no! Yes, maybe. But I don't want this guest to find out, he can tell my relatives and I will be in trouble. Is there anything you can do about it?'

'I am no magician as I cannot make him disappear as if he wore a cloak of invisibility. Nor, can I make him not notice that you like, sorry, who did you say? ...er.. this Sébastien'

Shanti was already starting to hate to have come to this man. Indeed, what was she expecting him to do? But her anxiety that she may be prevented from working at the villa was too much to endure. Not seeing Sébastien? No, that cannot be!

'I can give you a solution and some advice'

'Yes, anything!'

He lunged to the vase and grabbed a baby pink wild rose. Next, opened the chest on the floor, rummaged a bit, then brought a small box to the table. Taking a small sachet of paper, he started some incantations lighting an incense stick, turned to the framed deities on the wall, after which he handed it with the rose to Shanti.

'Take these, take all the petals of the flower, put in a bowl of water, add this powder, and rinse your face with it daily.'

'Morning or evening?'

'Morning, after you wash your face and brush your teeth. This person you don't want to know, will not recognize who you are, besides you could also not appear in front of him'.

'Are you sure, he will not recognize me?'

'If you did not believe in spiritual healing, you would not have come to me, would you?'

'Yes, indeed, I have no one to help me.'

'You can help yourself. Do what I told you, and if possible, don't go anywhere close to this man.'

Shanti was drinking his words, believing in the charm already. So, there it was! There was a solution. It was not for nothing that people in the village came to this man for solutions to their problems.

Of things one cannot tell anyone, of issues which offered no direct resolve. Healers have this special powder to create such solutions that work. Mintah had told her that her Mum could not handle her husband's drinking problem anymore. And that she went to a healer. After a week, he had stopped drinking, all of a sudden and never touched the bottle again.

Shanti left after giving the healer some money. She was convinced that what she was holding in her hand would work. She suppressed a shudder and quickly wiped a tear from the corner of her eye. She played the scenario of *Mawsi* finding out about her love for Sébastien.

'What are you talking about, idiot! Staff and labourers can't be friends! You're a coolie, and he's a white man. An Indian girl! You may be fairer than me, but that is nothing. You will never ever be anything other than a coolie! They will use you, and then throw you on the side when they are done. That's what white men do to poor people like us. You are a servant there. A servant, that's all!'

Shanti's vision blurred. Hot tears filled her eyes. This was a reality she was concealing to herself. She was behaving like an ostrich burying her head in sand. Full of love for a white man, her reason was not working, or did she stop seeing clearly? What is it with class, status and skin colour? Her Aunt had even brushed the whole marriage theme with her up to the wedding night, when Rishi's proposal had come forth. No one could understand why she was not willing to accept such a good party. She remembers clearly that conversation, when *Mawsi* cleared her throat and broached the subject of sex and marriage. No sooner did she start, she faltered. Her face turned crimson, she coughed before blurting out, "Your mother should have been here today. It's left to me now to tell you about all these things. Let me explain the facts of life to you. All I can say is that the wedding night is not very pleasant, but all women go through it. What to do? It's just something we have to put up with. Think! In return, you will have beautiful children and that will be your reward. A good husband of high caste, a house of your own, you will be a *maharani.*" She had pleaded with both her uncle and aunt not to marry her to Rishi. She found the man insipid.

"I don't want to leave home. I will work and earn more money for the family. Please don't send me away. Please, please I don't want to marry Rishi. Please don't make me." After some days of feeling and looking really miserable, *Mawsi* had sent a message to Rishi's father, that Shanti was still young, and she was not considering marriage just yet.

She heard the loud, drunken laughter of the men returning from the tea factory. Today was payday, and that meant many of them would be drunk on the cheap alcoholic drink, *arak*, sold at the local Chinese shop. Some would reach their home, staggering in their drunkenness and end up beating their wives or even children. It was fairly common, children and wives of the factory workers buried their suffering of an abusive father, with routine and tears.

She slowed down her steps, hid behind the tea

bushes and laid there till the voices and crude language faded into the distance. Clambering up the hill, she reached the villa with a quick foot, not to be spotted by anyone. Her Kajal had smeared from her tears, and her eyes were swollen from crying all the way.

*

The world was golden around and still, birds and insects resting in the final moments before dusk, when they would fill the air once more with their chaotic sounds and incessant movements.

Shanti slipped quietly through the iron gate. She made her way down the garden, the rain drizzled on the grass soaking her thin slippers, sending cold chills on her feet. Veronique was upstairs and didn't see her coming in. She went to wash her face and drink some water.

Maybe, she should use the rose and powder to start the magic immediately. She had to be patient and wait until next morning.

19 THE GREEN HEALER

'Live your life in such a way that every single morning when your feet hit the floor Satan shudders and says,' 'Oh Dear, she's awake!'

No continent, island, climate, or geography that is home to human culture lacks a formal tradition of incorporating local flora into daily and ceremonial life that was used as a means of enhancing health and well-being.

So, thought Devika when she welcomed the next day with some trepidation.

She had to finish her experimental decoctions of the past weeks. She was meticulously writing all the details in a notebook, sketching some drawings alongside.

Devika felt she had to come out triumphant in her struggle to make the tea estate successful. The idea of plying to an unknown investor to keep the place afloat was unthinkable. She has had many sleepless nights ruminating over what Me Noel had warned her about. And she ran into an epiphany thinking that even the worst troubles, always come with a solution.

What better way than to look home for one. Her Mother was a born herbalist and had passed on her knowledge to her only child. Devika. She has seen her mother time and again through the years, plant, nurture, use fruits, flowers, roots, barks, leaves of plants she discovered, with wonder, during each of the foraging walks she had had with her. People came to her for cures of ailments their doctor had abandoned. Some just trusted their mother first, then later, the doctor's medicine.

She remembered her mother's talks, which remain encrusted in her memory.

'Whatever your reasons for seeking balance you'll find that harmonizing yourself with the energy of nature can help you break free from the stressors in your life and focus on the here and now. And there is no better way to explore the bounty of nature than by following the path of the green healer. The way of the green healer is the path of the naturalist, the herbalist, and the healer. It is a free-form, flexible, and personalized practice for anyone who wants to explore the gifts of nature and use them to find balance and harmony in life. Remember, not everyone will be drawn to the same things and practice in the same way. It's about finding a workable balance in your own life within your own setting.

Nature has given us in its generous bounty, elixirs to all ailments, heartache and troubles in our body. Look around you, be attentive to what the bird sings, where it sits, what it eats, how the leaves rustle with the slightest breeze, how the beetle rolls a ball of soil bigger than itself, how does a lizard not fall despite walking upside down on the ceiling, and why does the bee drink so much nectar?

To the endless questions, are the endless answers. Nature answers them all. Teaches us anything if we are willing to listen. It's up to us to find these hidden answers. The path of the green healer is an intensely personal path that integrates ability, likes and dislikes, the climate of a particular geographic location, and interaction with the energy of that environment. It isn't a tradition so much as a personal adaptation of an ideal. I would like you, my girl, to one day remember and use all that I have taught you.'

Ever since, those words of wisdom rang again into her heart and mind, Devika started a quest of finding all the herbs and fruits around her. Her surroundings were bountiful. She just needed to extend her hand and get them. Her end goal was to mix them with tea and derive new flavours. Make the world discover new aromas with healing properties. Teas should be decoctions which make sense to balance the body rather than just quenching the thirst.

Her inheriting Bonne Espérance was no mere coincidence. There had to be something deeper to it. Otherwise, against all odds, how could she wake up each morning, look out of the window and believe all that stretched as far as the eye reached, belonged to her?

She was hell bent on rescuing the tea estate, and it made total sense that she had the green healing knowledge passed on by her mother. For it's about an individual choosing to harmonize her own life with the energy of nature.

Knowing yourself to be a part of a greater whole makes it difficult to act against that whole. Working with the earth means that to act against it would be counterproductive, and that includes acting against a member of the earth's extended energy, such as other people, animals, plants, and so forth. It is difficult to act unethically when you understand how everyone, and everything is affected by the negativity of such an action. If you love and respect the world around you, you will not abuse it. The more empathy and sympathy you have for your surroundings, the better you will treat them.

This is tied into the basic Golden Rule found in several religions. It's ethical reciprocity: if you treat those around you with courtesy, they will extend the same to you. What you put out into the world returns to you, and that goes for thoughts, acts, and energy. What goes around, comes around. With the well-tuned awareness that the green healer strives to possess comes a knowledge of who and what will be affected by her actions and choices. With this understanding, comes also the sense of responsibility and guardianship for life.

Devika jotted down a few herbs she had foraged earlier and penned a small poem too.

Lord and Lady,

Spirits of Nature,

Elements around me,

Bless me as I move through the world today.

May I bring joy and tranquillity to every life I touch.

May my actions bring only harmony to the world?

May I heal pain and soothe anger,

May I create joy and balance as I walk my path.

Support me and guide me, spirits of Nature,

This day and all days ahead of me.

This I ask of you, as a green witch,

And thank you for your many blessings.

Devika loved the decoction of bergamot with tea. It is a much-loved hot drink and well respected for its medicinal properties, in this part of the island. The citrus tang is just right for the tongue which sometimes loses its ability to taste, when nursing a fever or cold. Marcel, the gardener knows how to keep the bergamot trees in the garden well and healthy. Veronique never fails to get a few fruits to add to the basket, to squeeze in the tea.

Devika wrote:

'Bergamot (Citrus bergamia) is a pear-shaped citrus fruit grown primarily in Calabria, Italy, but also in Argentina, Brazil, Algeria, Morocco, Tunisia, Turkey, and parts of Asia. The rind of the green or yellow fruit is pressed for oil that is used for medicinal or dietary purposes. Some believe that the bergamot is a hybrid of lemon and bitter orange. The word "bergamot" is derived from a Turkish word that means "prince's pear."

Bergamot tea is not made solely from the fruit. Usually, it is made from black tea and bergamot extract. Also called Earl Grey tea, bergamot tea can be purchased with caffeine or without caffeine.

Earl Grey tea may also be produced using other tea leaves including green tea or rooibos tea. The amount of caffeine in the tea will depend on the leaves used to produce it.'

20 MEDICINAL HERBS

Devika went to dig out the old tin biscuit box from her chest of drawers. She kept old transcripts of her Mother in it. There was one which she consulted each month when her menses appeared. They had days and dates of a monthly calendar, and each spelled a prediction. If she got her period on a Sunday on the 10th, for example, it would read: 'glory and happiness. Caution with a close friend'.

So far, these predictions have never been false. She also had one on the languages of flowers. She loved the cursive handwriting of her mother and read it many times. She found the yellowed pages which read:

Flowers to express Love: Bergamot, gardenia, jasmine, lavender, rose.

Lust: basil, cinnamon, ginger, neroli, sandalwood, ylang ylang, patchouli Prosperity: almond, bergamot, honeysuckle, mint, peony, sage

Healing: Raspberry, carnation, mimosa, rosemary, sandalwood, chamomile, lavender

Protection: Sage, basil, frankincense, lavender, myrrh, cinnamon, pennyroyal

Luck: all spice, nutmeg, orange, violet,

Business/Money: Chrysanthemum, cinnamon, mint, peony.

Success: Geranium, cinnamon, bergamot, clove, ginger, lemon balm.

Happiness: Vanilla, almond, marjoram, cherry

Sleep: chamomile, lavender, violet.

Vitality: bay, carnation, pennyroyal, pepper, peppermint

Peace: jasmine lavender, gardenia, passionflower.

She decided to research more as to how she could derive new flavours for the teas with healing properties. Just like it is common knowledge that when you come down with a cold, many find it convenient to reach for an over-the-counter treatment, but these can have adverse side effects. What's worse, many of us may be unknowingly over-medicating ourselves and our children, thinking that if a small dose of a drug is good, then more is even better.

Herbal medicine provides a way to avoid the dangers of over-the-counter medicines, instead treating and healing common illnesses without all the synthetic ingredients. Whether you are experiencing insomnia, have a little one with itchy chicken pox, or find yourself dealing with an unexpected illness, it's likely that plant-based remedies can help.

Devika recalls how her mother would devote Saturdays as a purge, it was an all-day affair. She would be given castor oil to drink on an empty stomach early morning, followed by copious herbal teas of 'bigarade' - bergamot and ginger. No solid food intake for the whole day, lunch was a broth of moringa leaves. The action was fast and soon she would be visiting the toilet often, and by the end of the day, she felt light, but hungry.

When the season was changing, she would be given Tulsi - holy basil herbal tea with honey and a light dip of black tea. It was believed to relieve any quick cooling of the body when the North West trade winds started blowing. Similarly, ginger and honey candy drop were popped, to soothe the throat of an oncoming cold.

Traditional African medicine places an emphasis on herbal remedies, relying on a natural pharmacy that contains approximately 4,000 native plants. Even pharmaceutical companies recognize the importance of Africa's herbal medicines, learning from local practitioners and using traditional remedies to identify bioactive agents that can be used to prepare modern synthetic medicines. The slaves brought in their share of knowledge which became fused with other local ones enriching the landscapes of the subtropical plants with medicinal properties.

Minor digestive complaints such as indigestion and nausea often responded well to herbal remedies. A cup of peppermint or chamomile tea is sometimes all that's needed to help you feel more comfortable. Overburdened livers benefit, too, as many herbs provide protection and can even help restore normal function following injury or illness. Aloe Vera - *mazambron* is a well-known example of a cactus that can help keep your liver healthy besides treating burns and skin ailments. It also treats minor sprains, sore muscles, while painful joints can be targeted with internal and external herbal medicines. Internally, botanicals with high levels of antioxidants support the health of connective tissue; external poultices of turmeric and aloe Vera with arnica provide soothing comfort while eliminating bruises from injuries. Aloe vera gel contains antibacterial compounds that help prevent burns from becoming infected, and it also offers anti-inflammatory benefits. Aloe stimulates collagen synthesis, so skin regenerates faster after a minor burn. While it's strongest when taken fresh from the plant, bottled aloe gel will do at a pinch.

Devika often saw her mother using the bark of the moringa tree, as infusion with *Ayapana* for vaginal discomforts. Premenstrual syndrome (PMS), menopausal symptoms, and pregnancy side effects are often easier to manage when you know which herbs to use. She knew, from experience, how to give advice on their use. Ginger can help you deal with morning sickness, and both PMS and menopausal symptoms respond well.

Overeating, abdominal gas, and the onset of women's premenstrual cycles are a few of the things that can bring on an uncomfortable bout of bloating. Herbs help your body return to a more balanced state by supporting the elimination of toxins, excess gas, and built-up fluid. She would advise on taking a brew of fennel and peppermint when one has bloating. It provides comfort and quick relief. These pleasant-tasting plants contain strong antispasmodic agents that relax muscle tissue in the digestive tract. Adding a teaspoon of honey can help if the flavour of the tea is too strong.

Often the result of irritation, infection, or allergies, bronchitis occurs when the bronchial linings become inflamed. The condition is often characterized by a deep, rasping cough. Herbal treatments, combined with increased warm fluid intake and plenty of rest, have proven useful in reducing and eliminating the symptoms of bronchitis. Camphor rubs and as poultice are excellent for such an ailment. Many people unknowingly suffered from asthma too, until the attacks become too frequent to ignore. Much was due to the vast expenses of sugar cane plantation which have large inflorescences. When the harvest is near, there is a rise in allergies. Some chronic bronchial conditions, past allergies and asthma involve inflamed airways in the lungs, along with constricted bronchial tubes. Asthma attacks can be very frightening, so some people also experience panic attacks when breathing becomes difficult.

Chamomile contains a strong anti-spasmodic constituent, which relaxes tense, aching muscles and helps relieve the pain of colic. Its ability to calm stress and anxiety can help babies to sleep better. If breastfeeding, drinking chamomile tea helps ease baby's symptoms.

Many women came to ask for quick remedies, and they would always send back some fruits, and vegetables as a thank you token, after having been successfully healed.

Devika had not worked so hard against the clock. She wanted to taste all the brews with all the flavours she had gathered: fruits, herbs, roots, peels, barks and flowers. Veronique suggested she worked on the main kitchen table, in that way, she could help do the washing up after the countless pots of boiling, brewing and straining were done. Shanti was excited by all the herbs and the fragrance emanating from the kitchen. It looked like a real *champ de bataille*.

One which Devika wanted to win, at all cost.

21 MISTRESS

The stars were bright. The full moon shone like a gold disk. The constant screeching of crickets suddenly felt like music. Fireflies glittered in the tamarind tree beside the path. Their lights pulsed like the strings of light bulbs the tea pickers placed around a tree for Diwali.

This evening was slowly surpassing every other evening of her existence. The man of her dreams was standing beside her. His voice was gentler than she had ever heard it to be – it was almost as if he were breathing the words into her ear. The usual tone of authority and command had been replaced by one of inquiry and something else she was not quite sure about.

As a child, Shanti had once found an injured bumble bee crawling on the ground under a bush and felt sad for it. She had been sure it was going to die. Asha, her cousin had smiled and told her a story of bees getting drunk more on fragrance than on nectar. Shanti had not believed her, but now that she felt lightheaded and weak-kneed, she wondered if maybe her cousin's story carried some weight. Perhaps the scent of the jasmines and lilies had intoxicated her... or perhaps, it was the nearness of the man.

The sound of an old gramophone playing some French music, floated in the air, cooled by a breeze ruffling the sheer curtains. Shanti stood silently savouring the moment to its fullest and memorizing all the sensations for a recall, later. Such a moment might never be repeated again. Her skin tingled all over; her heart beat hard against her chest. Her nerves were on edge, waiting for something to happen. Sébastien looked incredibly handsome tonight. He had donned a light flowery cotton shirt with short sleeves, revealing a pair of arms where the mark of white skin demarcated sharply against his tanned biceps. A pair of calico linen trousers completed his look, revealing his lean body. His golden hair combed while still wet gave a slick look. His deep blue eyes shone each time he looked at Shanti.

Catching a moment when no one was looking, he leaned by her side and whispered, 'You haven't answered my question,' he gently reminded her. 'Which question?' she asked, suddenly looking lost and confused.

'What sort of person is your aunt?'

'I told you *Missier*, she is a nice person'

'Then she is not the type to chase me with a stick if I ask for your hand?'

The look of surprise and disbelief in Shanti's

eyes pleased Sébastien. Other tea pickers giggled, nudged each other, and even made thinly veiled offers of sexual pleasures to him, if she ever talked to them. They laughed rollickingly at his discomfort and embarrassment as he would beat a hasty retreat.

But this girl... This girl was different.

She loved him, no doubt. And he needed to be loved. His physical need for her became almost a pain that seared through his body and made his head spin. The loneliness of the last months must have caught up with him, for he suddenly wrapped her hand in his. She did not draw back. Nobody was watching. Veronique hummed while getting the next course ready, while Devika and Rishi were at the end of the verandah, discussing. The dinner hosted by the mistress of the house was a tantalising occasion to get to know Rishi the tea taster and show him her experiments. Devika certainly was making the best of the time, not missing any detail in her conversation with Rishi.

Sébastien's mind was clamouring to get closer to Shanti. Since he got her to work at the villa, he had not had a single moment when he could talk to her, alone.

'Shanti?'

'Oui, *Missier*.'

'Will you come to my room tonight?'

'Why? Do you need something?'

'No, I am just asking you to be with me. Please come, you know what I am asking of you?'

'Yes...' Shanti just looked down at the floor, blushing to the roots of her hair.

When dawn broke the next morning, Shanti tiptoed back to her room. She knew she was right from day one. Sébastien loved her as much as she loved him. She had lost her innocence to him. She could not push him away, when he amorously held her in his arms.

Her passion for him burned and consumed them both.

According to local customs, she was no longer eligible for marriage. She trusted Sébastien when he said that he would ask for her hand. However, the fear of being called a mistress to a white man made her feel queasy and left a bad taste in her mouth.

*

Many managers and white masters had mistresses. It was a custom frowned upon by most tea pickers and planters, but it was tolerated and even joked about among both men and women. They understood a man's loneliness but considered the practice as exploitation, by the rulers of the ruled. There was a long tradition of powerful men taking women from the poorer or lower classes. They had an equally long tradition of ostracizing the women, who, in most cases, had been used and then abandoned. The society persisted in calling them women without honour. Shanti feared she had shamed all the workers on the estate. Sébastien had not forced her. He could be forgiven, somehow, but she could not. The workers knew that when the white men grew tired of their native mistresses, the women were returned to their houses, where they faced mudslinging and ridicule for the rest of their lives. The women labelled them "whores"; the men made lewd propositions. The temporary lover may give his woman a few trinkets, but these gifts invariably would dry up when the man finds someone new. No one called it an affair or love.

Shanti would not be able to face the anger of her *Mawsa* and Mausi. Not even Mintah. She fought back her tears. The community's and relatives' rejection might be a price Shanti would have to pay for the fulfilment of her love, no matter how short. Her lover not only belonged to a different class and religion but was a foreigner as well.

Her life right now had stopped yet began at the same time.

She had washed her face with the rose in water and the powder added to it. Rishi so far, had not noticed her. Could it be the dim candlelight? Or was Devika her saviour? For she had not left Rishi for one moment being in intense discussion while sat on the verandah, sipping their drinks and eating snacks.

A week later, Shanti visited her *Mawsi*. She had made up her mind to come out honestly about her love affair. She would not like that her folks learnt about it from others.

The distance was not much, but it was arduous for the woman whose legs now got used to polished floors rather than beaten earth and steep slopes. She argued with herself about the pros and cons of the visit before she rose and resolutely continued on her way to the house where *Mawsi* lived. Shanti could not think of the proper words to say to start the conversation. Reaching the entrance, she stepped back and stood in the middle of the gravel path. *Mawsi* saw her first.

'Shanti, well that's a surprise! I was not expecting you'

'Namaste *Mawsi*, yes, I had a short break and thought I wanted to visit you. How have you all been?'

'We are good, but I miss you. Would you like some tea? I made some *thekua* yesterday.'

'*Mawsi*, I have something to tell you ...' Her aunt's face dulled for a moment. She looked at Shanti.

And then, just like that, she spilled the truth.

'This is not what I meant when I advised you to choose a young man to marry. Rishi was good for you. Had you accepted, today you would not have been in this situation. Hey Bhagwan! Why did I let you go and work there?'

'I can't help it. I have loved him since the first time I saw him. It seems it was the same for him too' she pleaded.

'You think that it is a great privilege to be chosen by a white, but it is not. He will never marry you. If he does, he will not rise above his present position in the tea company. He will lose all his white friends. They will never accept you, and your people will never stop spitting at you, for being a mistress.'

Shanti did not answer. She did not hang her head with shame as Mawsi had expected. But the word 'mistress' stung hard.

'Have you lost all sense of pride? I have known you all your life. Have you forgotten about your own Mother's fate? I helped your mother during your birth and cared for you from the day you were orphaned. Now, after you have sinned, you dare look straight into my eyes like an honest person! You have shamed your *Mawsa* and me.' She wept for a few minutes and then rose to leave.

Shanti stepped forward with open arms to hug her.

'Don't touch me!'

Shanti held an outstretched hand and took a quick step backwards. She stumbled, took some more steps backwards before she regained her balance. Her breath turned into short, quick pants. Her heart pounding, she gasped to recover and breathe normally again. Her eyes flooded with tears once more, and she spoke softly.

'My father was a white too,' she said. 'My mother suffered because of him. I know what my future will be, but I love this man, and I am willing to pay the price that a few days of happiness with him will demand. He is my *devta*. You have to believe me Mawsi, I have not sinned, we are in love.'

'*Devta*! Huh," *Mawsi* scoffed. 'Gods demand

devotion as their right and are condescending in their gifts to you. If your man is your *devta*, mark my words, he will make a slave out of you. When I think that you refused a life of respectability from Rishi, to give yourself to this French man.'

After a few moments of silence, Shanti asked, 'the photo in that metal frame on the sideboard .... Is that of my father?'

'Yes. I kept it so that one day, you will know who your father is. I understand now why you want to be with white people. It must be blood calling out to blood. Why do you think your mother pretended to be a widow? It was safer for her reputation, so that people did not call you a bastard. Poor woman, after all that suffering and sacrifice. All this, for love. Now, my girl, you are walking in the same steps as your mother.'

In spite of *Mawsi's* earlier words and derisive looks, nothing had penetrated the bubble of happiness that surrounded Shanti. In some ways, it felt like a complete break with the past and a final farewell to her aunt. *Mawsi* gave all her mother's belongings. When Shanti objected, *Mawsi* said that if her Devta abandoned her, she would have nothing to live for, anyway. The river was not far. Besides the pair of gold bangles, some brass plates, a few lace blouses and some sarees, there was not much she would keep.

Shanti sat outside for a while, collecting her thoughts. Suicide?! No. Many women have been in the situation she is now, threatened by it, but when the time came, the instinct for survival almost always had an edge over the fear of the unknown.

Besides, she was in a mindset to want to live, not to die. She had just started living a dream, one where Sébastien held her in his arms, whispered sweet words of love to her, and she stroked his soft golden hair while looking into his deep blue eyes.

When Shanti made a move to go, she discovered that her anxiety had waned, while her affection for her aunt had not diminished at all. There was a calmness, similar to one when a cyclone's eye passes over, before fretting even more fiercely. She did not know what awaited her in her future with Sébastien, but she was willing to face it. She held Mawsi's hand while the latter offered a last piece of advice.

'Promise me that you will take care of yourself and live each moment to the fullest, as this will not last. Your *Missier* will leave you and marry a white woman as soon as he has enough of you. You will find yourself warming your heart with memories, like we try to warm ourselves around a *chulha's* dying embers, on cold nights. One side gets warm while the other stays cold. Then, even the embers stop glowing. Please, don't get pregnant. Go to the pharmacy and get some pills.'

'*Mawsi*, pills?! How am I to ask that, seeing I

am not married? Word will spread like wildfire that I am sleeping with someone.'

'You can always say it's for me. Everyone knows that I have had a difficult pregnancy and almost died when Asha was born. And taking precautions is the next natural thing to do. You can never trust men to take their responsibility. Now, that you are grown up, I can tell you these things easily. Go my girl and may *bhagwan* be with you.'

Shanti stood on the entrance with a growing sense of sadness as she looked at her only well-wisher in the world, wiped her tears away while bidding her goodbye. She sincerely hoped that her aunt's predictions would not come true.

22 MA CHERIE

Shanti was superstitious. For the Hindus, auspicious dates were set for weddings and the night a marriage was consummated. All chosen by an astrologer after he had consulted various charts, including the couple's horoscopes and the positions of the stars. Even people unconnected with the couple were careful not to say things that could be considered a bad omen or could be interpreted by evil spirits as permission to play mischief and cause unhappiness. Shanti had given herself to Sébastien without a wedding ceremony, as she thought of nothing at the time. Now, all the details of caution were flashing in her mind. She hoped that the stars had been lined up in the heavens in a way that would ensure happiness for them both. *Mawsi* had meant well, but from what she said, Shanti was doomed to a lonely old age if Sébastien did not marry her. After all, she had started her new life with a man by losing the only thing of value that she possessed.

On her way to the villa, Shanti wondered how *Mawsi* would break the news to her husband. *Mawsa* would probably vow that she never sets foot into their house again. From where she stood, Shanti knew that her life was in the hands of Sébastien now.

Another problem loomed. How will she conceal their affair from Devika and Veronique, the rest of the workers at the villa, the world? Shanti was too tired to think anymore.

She went straight to her room upon reaching the villa. Washed her face and collected herself. Now, it all depended on Sébastien and herself.

If they were lucky, life could be a joy. Otherwise, there was always the river or the ocean, as *Mawsi* had suggested.

*

Sébastien had heard much talk about the temptation of willing and beautiful local girls. Their seduction, he had heard, was deadly. He had been similarly warned by almost every old sweat he met. He understood his situation very well. He met with Paul and was surprised that the manager already knew about his relationship with Shanti.

‘It is rare in our custom to recognize the children of such unions,’ Paul said lighting a fag. ‘They may be accepted in France, but out here, we are in charge, and we just do not fraternize with the labourers.’ Forgetting that he was a *mulâtre* himself, a half bred.

‘If the word spread, you would not be welcome at the *hippique* club, the swimming pool, sporting events, or anywhere else where whites socialise. You probably should stop seeing this woman. It is none of my business, just friendly advice.'

'Honestly, I do not know from where you got all this, and I fully take my responsibility, if you want to know my opinion. I am not to hide cowardly behind colonial ill-practices and prejudices. If I love a woman, that's my personal business, but thank you for your concern. I appreciate it, Paul.'

Sébastien thought of the manager's words as he rode back home. He handed the jeep over to Marcel and went into the house to wash and change for dinner. Shanti was standing at the desk, leafing through a coffee table book on India she picked from the teak bookshelf laden with old books. She was completely absorbed. Sébastien looked over her shoulder. The book was open to a page that showed an elephant hunt. Men on the backs of trained elephants were herding wild elephants into a wooden enclosure. Some were beating drums and burning torches helping to frighten the animals. The wild herd looked terrified.

Sébastien gently blew on the nape of Shanti's neck. She had not heard him come in.He now got used to walking barefoot around the house. She turned around with a bright smile but did not embrace him as he had expected her to. Instead, she returned her gaze to the book.

'What is it you find so interesting?' he asked. 'More interesting than me?'

'I don't understand how they can do such a thing. These elephants once roamed the jungle and then had their freedom taken away. How can they help trap other elephants into captivity? They have long memories so they should remember how frightening and cruel their training period was, right? People are not afraid that Lord Ganapati would be angry and punish them? They worship our elephant god for everything and yet torture real ones like that?'

'They have become good servants to men,' Sébastien patiently explained. 'They do whatever their masters ask them to do, even if it means forgetting who they are and where they came from. Their love and loyalty are dedicated to their mahouts and nobody else.'

Shanti Looked at him, her eyes flickering with sadness caused by his words. But she recovered from it very quickly with a shy smile.

'Do you mean that they are happy doing what they do, and that men should manipulate them like this? This is cruel. Enslaving a wild animal, separating it from its family, shackling it and making it work like this? Do you find it right?'

Shanti thought, this is what happens when culture clashes. When one does not worship Bhagwan Ganapathy. When one sees an animal just as a vehicle for labour. Similar to people who choose to be enslaved and work for their masters. Like in the sugar and tea plantations. Like herself. There was no difference between herself and the captured elephant.

Sébastien pulled her hand away from the book

and kissed her fingers. She pulled them away immediately.

'Not here, someone might see us!'

'So what? We are in love. It's not an offense.'

'What if Madame Devika saw us, she would sack me immediately.'

'You still don't know Devika, do you? She will be the last person to repudiate you. Don't worry about anybody. You are my Cherie now'

Sébastien left for his room, leaving Shanti euphoric once more in two days. He called her his 'Cherie' and said not to worry about anyone. *Mawsi* should have heard that, she would realise that maybe not all white men are abusers.

23 TEA BLENDS

'My own life has been so enriched by herbs and herbal teas that I want to share my enthusiasm with you. Like many people, I've tried herbs in myriad forms, but I can honestly say that I haven't found another way to take herbal remedies for health treatments that can match the simplicity, grace, and effectiveness of herbal teas.' Devika said while tucking her saree *pallu* around her waist.

She had called Rishi again, after the last dinner. It was a shame that Sébastien could not join in. She noticed that he remained hovering around Shanti lately.

Rishi nodded in approval, happy that the Mistress had taken to appreciate his unique skills and talent as a tea taster.

'It's not for nothing that tea has been called the plant of Heaven. For 4,000 years, it's been valued both as a medicine and a drink for pleasure. And look .... Rishi, we are blessed with acres of this magnificent plant. Isn't it marvellous?! It is time we gave it to the world, the magic of this plant.'

'Yes, Madame, we have been doing so for years'

'But we have not revealed secret flavours with healing powers in our tea! That's what we need to do. Hippocrates said, "Thy food shall be thy medicine," and herbs, as concentrated foods with vital nutrients, vitamins, and medicinal properties, more than fit the bill. In Hippocrates' time, herbs were the official medicines. We have our tea. That should be our medicine.'

'I fully agree Madame. But we have to be cautious.'

'Cautious? About what? No, in fact we need to promote our products better. Sébastien will need to work on a better marketing strategy and send some samples to the tea auctioneers.'

Devika was very excited. She believed in the natural wonder of Bonne Espérance.

'Teas are herbal drinks, and because of that, they can do much more than quench your thirst or calm you after a long day. Teas are the ideal way to get the healing power of herbs into your everyday diet. Drugless remedies. Natural energy. Pure and simple drinks that can provide effective herbal defences against disease. I'd like to introduce you to the wonderful world of herbal and flavoured teas with special healing properties. Taste them each and tell me what you think. There's power in those flowers, leaves, roots, rhizomes, berries, seeds, and bark—positive plant energy that is absorbed easily and gently through teas. There are immunity-building teas to strengthen your body's own natural defences, or to rebuild your strength after antibiotics, illness, or surgery. There are stress reducers, nervous-system soothers, and anti-anxiety teas. Imagine how this would help the community of our tea pickers. Herbal teas are a valuable resource for people who don't want to rely on pills for minor discomforts and ills.'

Rishi had a long day of tasting and spitting. Veronique and Shanti were amused. They made lunch adhering to the strict guidelines of no onion, garlic or any pungent spices in the food. Hence, a plain watercress bouillon was served with an equally plain mashed potato, and mint-coriander tomato chutney. No harm to those delicate taste buds.

Devika carried on writing in her notebook, deriving more information from her Mother's old books and diaries. She found a yellowed page which wrote: "Better to be deprived of food for three days than of tea for one - *Ancient Chinese Proverb*" where was scribbled *v. Imp.* She had registered all that she could possibly think of and found to rebrand tea from Bonne Espérance. The notes soon filled the pages, there was no stopping Devika. She was a trailblazer, a determined trait inherited from her mother.

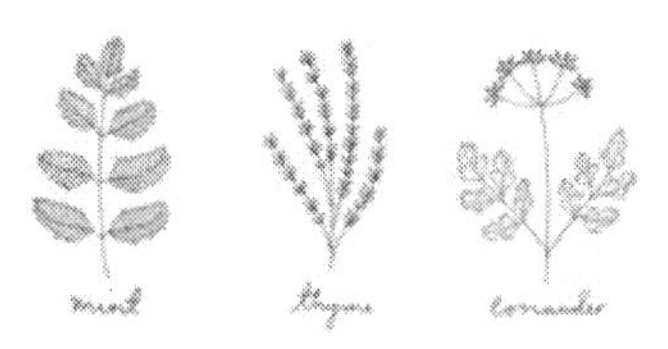

Devika continued to read and make notes. Herbs are not magic potions reserved for dark rooms, musty shelves, and coloured bottles. They're plants that grow in sun or shade; some flowers, some bear fruit, some are showy, others are plain, some are woody, and others seemingly dull. In the roots, leaves, flowers, berries, bark, or seeds, herbs have specific properties that are healing and restorative for our systems. Moringa seeds, for instance, have naturally occurring calcium.

That's good news for people who need calcium and aren't milk drinkers. Those who need to prevent fluid retention but can't afford the potassium losses common to standard diuretics can take *Angelica sinensis*, a fragrant plant with a cluster of small white flowers. The flower belongs to the same botanical family as carrots and celery. It is rich in vitamin E and minerals for a vital energy tonic that can be exceptionally good for menopausal women. Herbs do their job because of the properties they contain. There's no magic in it, just biochemistry.

The unique value of herbs in herbal teas, is that it is the most effective way to get the benefits of herbs, safely and easily. She continued to read and absorb.

UNCOMPROMISED VALUE

Herbal teas are true natural resources. They have no additives, preservatives, or chemical dyes. They aren't sweetened with sugar or sugar substitutes, and they're not mixed with other ingredients that could compromise the herb's effect. There are many which are caffeine free.

EASY ABSORPTION

The water in herbal teas plays a vital role to increase the effectiveness of the remedy. Water is essential for the absorption and assimilation of nutrients. The water diffuses the potency of the herb and delivers its properties in a manner that is harmonious with the body's natural processes.

Unlike herbal capsules that never touch the taste buds, herbal teas follow the normal digestive process from the mouth through the digestive system, which is an automatic regulator for substances entering the body.

Many herbs can come in premeasured tea bags that take the guesswork out of measuring herbs. If there was one thing that Devika was thrilled doing was researching, writing, even painting the medicinal teas and tea blends.

Shanti blossomed. Away from *Mawsi* and with her newfound love and freedom of life on the tea estate, she gained confidence. She looked taller, slimmer and with cheeks often as red as a *roussaille* - Surinam cherry. Her body took on the curves of a young woman that were difficult to conceal. Her soft brown eyes shone with health. Love was shining from her in the open without caution of the outside world.

Devika's written notes grew lengthy in tune with her creative juices. She was understanding how she could sail Bonne Espérance's future towards modernity.

She carried on writing a short presentation to give to Sébastien. He had to know about all her findings and new ideas.

'The taste of an herbal tea made from fresh herbs is exhilarating. If the herb comes from your own garden, it gives you a sense of satisfaction, that is unbeatable. Peppermint, for instance, is so aromatic that you get invigorated just with a snap of a leaf.

Plant peppermint in your garden to have iced peppermint tea on a hot December day. Freeze the herb fresh, or dry it for future use, to have warm peppermint tea in winter.

You can make your teas from fresh garden herbs but keep these precautions in mind: Never pick herbs in the wild to use for teas, since you cannot know whether the area was sprayed with chemical insecticides.

Make sure a neighbouring plant isn't woven into the herb you are picking, since plants tend to be friendly with each other.

Be sure to use the correct parts of the plant for your tea. Each herb has specific parts that are used for their healing properties.

For instance, only use flower petals for

chamomile but for mint tea you can use the whole plant above the root.

The beauty of Tea-Blends

One tea a day is better than none.

Two teas a day are better than one.

The beauty in a cup of blended tea is the extra boost of healing that an additional herb can bring. Blends provide a way for you to individualize your herbal teas. You can create flavours that are richer than the original brew, aromas that elevate your mood as you sip your tea, and you can create synergy - combination of flavour and energy that literally sparkles with health benefits.

You can make a plain tea tantalizing, a bitter tea sweet, a tart tea mellow, and you can take a tonic tea to flow gently through your system like a quiet river. As you get to know the healing virtues in the variety of herbs that are used for teas, you'll probably find that you prefer some herbs over others for their unique tastes. They provide a means for you to create herbal teas that are inspired by your own tastes and desires and suited to your particular health needs. You can express your individuality in your own blends.

24 MASTERS

‘Don’t we have to rethink packaging?’ Rishi advanced.

‘Of course, but what’s best is that we do them in biodegradable packaging. In that way, we make sure we are not polluting the planet. Herbs may come dried in tea boxes, or you can buy them by the ounce from herb shops. Preparing tea from bulk, is easier than you think. After a while, you’ll learn to love this method because you can make your brew exactly the way you like it.’ Devika explained to Rishi.

She worked day and night, grateful that she was well looked after, and that her baby was loved by both Shanti and Veronique who doted on her. She decided to illustrate her ideas and supplement her creative experiments. She went downtown to get some art materials and she set to work immediately. The verandah was the perfect spot to spread out her notes, enjoy the changing light of the day and cool shade to paint.

She was a watercolourist but never had time to use her skills enough. She started with all the flowers and leaves she could gather in the garden. She saw her blends from an aesthetic perspective, in the same way she saw the merging colours of sunsets, trees, and stones on the paths in her paintings.

She created a colour wheel by selecting her herbs for their healing value, and with blends for their richness of tones. She uses different hues for different seasons, as if she's drinking the blend, the colour was her inspiration.

Red and purple blends for winter -Devika uses berry teas like *Roussaill*e for their sweet and tangy bitter taste, wild strawberry, and raspberry to colour winter blends. These are herbs that are rich in minerals and vitamin C to fight colds and flu, and keep the body tuned throughout the cold months. They combine radiantly with plain-tasting herbs.

Bright green and yellow blends for summer - her selections were light, cleansing herbs like chamomile, parsley, and peppermint which make fabulous iced teas. They're packed with nutritious elements and give the system a fresh, clean feeling to breeze through summer with renewed energy. They harmonize with each other or brighten a plain brew.

Deep green and amber blends for all year round, with choices as the woody teas like cinnamon bark and apple. Both make a marvellous infection fighter, and one cinnamon stick is the equivalent of one herb in a blend. Add a cinnamon stick to an amber brew and you get an "aromatic topaz."

The long spell of the rainy season in the high plateau with the light, intermittent rains, made the villa of la Bonne Espérance seem almost enjoyable to Shanti. Amidst the black clouds, flashes of sheet lightning illuminated the dark sky, and the torrents did not let up for weeks. Small streams became raging floods. The nights were heavy with humidity and the frogs croaked, seeking mates. But the house did not leak, unlike at her *Mawsi's* place where she had to get the buckets and pails ready as soon as the distant thunders were heard. Here, her feet remained dry, and felt warm. No more mucking in mud.

Anthills exploded in fireless volcanoes, just after sunset, and a cloud of winged ants rose into the air, only to be devoured by all sorts of birds.

Marcel, the gardener, sometimes doused the anthills with alcohol and lit them with a matchstick. This prevented unpleasant surprises of a red ant climbing up one's leg and biting with its fiery sting. Mosquitoes were not abundant here as much as ants. The cool climate inhibited them, but one was never devoid of red ants and long-legged ones which packed even more venom. Marcel called them '*gangalo*' which rather gave a comical tone to these not-to-mess-with ants. The island, fortunately, did not have any more native baddies. There were no snakes, but a local *couleuvre* which was benign and measured only a foot long. No creepy crawlies, no ferocious animals, either. The virginal island was intact as it had originally only inhabited by some birds and the famous Dodo before it was decimated to extinction. Dogs, rats, mongoose, tenrecs, hens, and goats were brought by the French settlers when they started the sugar cane fields. Apparently, mongoose is a fierce hunter of rodents. This made walking barefoot in the tea estates completely harmless. No leeches, no snakes, no other venomous creatures.

Shanti had been close to nature when she lived with her Aunt in La Chartreuse. She felt close to *Bhagwan*, each of his creations striking a chord somewhere within her. She was burning incense with *loban* in a small terracotta burner, swirling it around each room of the house. She believed this drove evil spirits away. She was worried that her love for Sébastien and her blissful life caught some evil eye.

'What are you doing Shanti? Don't get close to the baby please, with all that smoke' Devika said while dipping her brush in the glass of water, concentrating on her watercolour.

'Do not worry Madame, baby is fine. This is to remove *'hai' mauvais lizier*.'

Devika did not reply. She treated everyone fairly, and never intervened in the general running of the house. She trusted them, and they in return served her with devotion. The only response to her kindness should be gratitude and not meaningless demands.

Whites lived in grand villas like this one, while other people inhabited a different world from theirs. *Mawsi* told Shanti of the time the white folk had complete control over the life and death of their workers.

The indentured workers could not even run away. Wardens roamed the lines at night to make sure of this. The masters had learnt their lessons from the *esclaves marrons*, and they could not afford to lose the *girmityas* too. The employees were always in debt and had to toil ceaselessly, till every last cent owed to the masters, had been paid off. Those who were suspected of malingering, were flogged. After much protest, the laws were changed, and a magistrate was appointed to deal with each case individually. The whites did not like to be accused of injustice in front of other fellow families. The workers now cowered before the magistrate in addition to grovelling before the white planters. Although the fines imposed were lighter and cruel measures like flogging were abolished, a magistrate's judgment would nearly always favour a planter. Times were changing.

Shanti believed that she was never going to be accepted as one of their kind even though she could become Sébastien's wife. But that had not happened yet. If any white person ever did something for her, even by accident, she should just accept it with humility and gratitude, as if from the gods.

Nobody really liked their children being of dusky skin, the fairer the better. And having an offspring from Sébastien would at least mean her child would be fairer than any on the tea estate.

Devika was not white, but she lived in a villa, owned acres of, she had servants, driver, gardener, tea pickers by the hundreds, factory employers, and even Sébastien, a French man, as general manager of the tea estate. She was unimaginably lucky. The woman never showed an ounce of arrogance nor haughtiness. In fact, she was very humble, quiet, and compassionate. However, she held a heavy sadness in her heart.

She spent time with her baby girl each day, but then would not see her for long hours. This intrigued both Shanti and Veronique. While they both felt they needed to replace that void by giving as much affection to the baby as they could, between them. Devika never spoke of her husband nor was there any visible picture of them both displayed around the house. What was the secret? Did Devika also share her own misfortune of having a white husband who abandoned her and her child?

Mawsi's words of caution did not completely kill Shanti's curiosity about her father. She had closely watched her friends' fathers during the years. Most were very protective of their daughters. They often spanked their sons but seldom struck their daughters. Girls seemed to be precious, but they were only temporary guests in their parents' homes; they needed a lot of love since they were not sure of the homes they were going to be married into. Needless to say, Shanti felt a bit envious of these girls.

When she had asked about why her own father left her mother, during that recent conversation about her affair with Sébastien, *Mawsi* had replied,

'He wanted a white child. You were brown,'

This brutal honest reality hit her in the face. It all suddenly made sense to her why fairer girls were always preferred than dusky ones. The skin colour made a huge difference. Whether your own father accepts you or not. But she was not entirely convinced; she believed that her father would love his daughter if only he got the chance to meet her. She had his blood in her veins, after all. Though her aunt never fuelled Shanti's imagination about her father, the little girl's secret desire turned into dreams of meeting the man she could call 'father'. She kept this deep feeling and expectation from everyone else.

She was made to understand that her life would be incomplete without a husband, a home, and children. Shanti received a rudimentary education for five years in a school the planters had started for the tea-garden children. The first lesson was a long talk given by the garden doctor about the importance of boiling drinking water. She learnt how to read and write in English and French.

She would have liked to have drawing classes but there were none. Art was considered a waste of time. Halfway through the sixth year of schooling, she decided that she had had enough. The teacher was dull and repetitive. To add to that, he was also harsh and did not hesitate to use his rattan cane frequently on the children's tender skins. Parents thought that was the rule and had no reason to complain, and the management did not bother to stop him. He spent most of his time combing his scanty strands of oiled hair with a small comb which remained in his pocket at all times. He did not show any interest in the students which seemed a bit slow, but instead put them to sit at the back of the class. A denial to himself, that they even existed.

When Shanti refused to go to school and stubbornly stood her ground, *Mawsi* did not force her to continue. Most of Shanti's friends had left already. They had begun helping their families with simple chores including collecting firewood, caring for their younger siblings, while others joined the classes at the village council hall on sewing, embroidery, baking, and basket making. Mintah learnt from there too. *Mawsa* suggested Shanti should join the afternoon *baitka* classes to learn Hindi and recite Ramayana verses. Girls who could do both were coined virtuous. Perhaps Shanti could do with some virtue added to her growing up as an orphan. A good party would be a good match if people saw those 'virtues' in her. *Mawsi* gave deaf ears to such suggestions. She believed in a girl learning practical skills. *Mawsa* never asked again. And Shanti never sat on the bench of the *baitka*. Maybe, there was a reason in the grand scheme of things. She was to live in France, speak French to a French husband, raising his French children. Hindi was an omission in her life.

25 VERONIQUE

'Shanti come here ...' Devika summoned gently.

The young girl moved closer to her and stood waiting.

'May I ask you something?'

'Sure, Madam'

'Are you in love?'

Shanti felt her head go around in a split of a second, the ground giving way under her feet. How did Devika know?

'No. non. Madame, why?'

'I just know. I would like you to tell me who it is, and if there is any way I can help? You are under my responsibility now; your welfare is important to me? Devika continued with a soft voice.

'What can I say Madame? It's complicated. Am not sure you will understand.'

'Try me .... or is it Sébastien?'

Shanti turned away and left. She could not reply to the Mistress. Acknowledging would be too risky, while lying was something Shanti was not willing to do.

*

There were certain days when the weather seemed to match one's mood. The sky cleared at around three o'clock, just in time for the end of Veronique's shift, and the clouds made way for the sun. She had a long line of laundry out, all white linen made whiter with a bit of the indigo square *'dibler'*.

Veronique had lately found Shanti a bit quiet and dismissive. The latter seemed to retreat by herself in her room. And come out whenever

Sébastien was here. She always hovered around him, asking to take his platter of morning coffee to his room. Veronique knew something was going on, but she was in denial. Her instincts coupled with her own infatuation with Sébastien were enough to stop her asking any questions.

Bonne Espérance's location, between the tropical green hills leading all the way down to the sea. Between workers dwellings burst forth luxuriant palms, thickets of bamboo, banana plants, vines, tropical ferns, breadfruit trees, and a whole host of other colourful flora. The most impressive of these was a tree that must have been at least fifty feet tall and consisted of a single trunk from which extended a fan of branches tipped with small palm leaves. The - Ravenala, or the 'traveller's palm'. Water was enclosed in its cluster of leaves trapped from rain, and when travellers could not find a source of water to quench their thirst, they would climb up the trunk, and collect it from there.

The air was pleasantly cool in the morning; the heat of the sun was already making itself felt, but the air was free of its usual stuffy humidity. Veronique went to get some money from Devika. She was going to Port Louis for some shopping. She was intending to pay a quick visit to an acquaintance too, if she had enough time. Sébastien had asked her to make ragout for him. She would try to get some *cabri* mutton from the grand bazar.

'Veronique do you mind getting me some chintz fabric from la rue la Corderie? I want to make some dresses for the baby for Summer. Select some pastel shades and some cotton baby lace for the collar. Try to find some very thin satin ribbons too.' Devika took a pause to speak to Veronique. She was bent on finishing her notes to present to Sébastien tonight.

'Yes, Madame, as you please. I have made

lunch; Shanti shall serve you today.'

'Don't worry, take your time.'

Veronique arrived in the city by bus. She got down and was soon swarmed by a wide thoroughfare of shops, offices and restaurants, arcaded pavements busy with street vendors. Crowded with taxis honking to get ahead faster, the streets looked busier than usual.

In the indoor part of the Grand Bazar, vegetable sellers hailed in loud voices pronouncing how fresh their produce was, mounds of green cress, chayote greens and herbs copiously sprayed with water to keep them fresh, made the floor wet and slippery. Outside were sellers with small glass caddies on bicycles busy selling *gâteaux patate*, wild scarlet raspberries, mounds of ripened yellow and ruby *goyaves de Chine*, *thekua*, pink candy floss, while women in bright saris sheltered themselves with multicoloured parasols balancing their heavy bags of groceries. A tinsmith clanked his hammer among an array of tin products hanging on his door. This is from where the putu sellers got their putu steamers made, bespoke strainers, cake tins, milk caddies, *caraye, dekchi,* household appliances, teapots and ladles.

Veronique took to the street which was the textile Mecca of the capital. One could find almost any fabric and haberdashery there. She browsed a few shops after stopping at a window, which caught her eye. From a distance, a blue midnight blue dress on a slender mannequin looked as though it had been cut from one single piece of silk. Its graceful lines draped and flowed would have accentuated her slim waist. The dress had been pieced together from scraps and offcuts, sewn edge to edge so cleverly that they had been transformed into something else. If only she had the opportunity, she would gladly join in an atelier of seamstresses. She made her own dresses but would have loved to be able to design, style and sew all sorts of garments. She continued to think about the possibility of a life elsewhere, filled with elegance and sophistication. She had concentrated on making her stitches smaller and neater, sewing quickly but fastidiously whenever she sewed anything. Her longing for pretty things was a form of escapism from her rough and ready upbringing in a small house with no windows. She shrugged off the feeling, telling herself that wallowing in self-pity wasn't going to help anyone. She moved on from her dreams, to the next shop where she purchased some fabrics Devika had requested.

She moved to her favourite shop. It was an Aladdin's cave. It sold practically everything–fresh vegetables, frozen foods, dried provisions, stationery, toiletries–all under one roof, a marked contrast to the open markets that people normally used. She usually purchased some piping hot steamed buns from here. Seeing her, the seller did not even ask what she wanted but swiftly packed four hot buns and handed them to her.

When Veronique reached home, Shanti was cooking. She was humming an old Hindi song, while stirring a pot of dal with sousou.

'Mmmm.... smells good!'

'Oh, you are back, how was Port Louis?'

'The usual, crowded, noisy, hot and I have a headache, but I brought some hot steamed buns for us.'

'Why don't you go and rest, while I finish cooking. We can have the buns tomorrow.'

'But they are fresh, still hot, by tomorrow they will not be so good.' Protested Veronique.

'Don't worry, I can carefully heat them, and we can have a breakfast of steamed buns, and lots of hot coffee, brewed black and heavily laced with condensed milk. We love that, don't we? When Madam is not looking, we would slurp the last remains at the bottom of the cup, using our spoons, sometimes even our fingers.'

Veronique got nearer to Shanti, 'thank you Shanti ... tell me, what's going on between you and Sébastien?'

Shanti turned around swiftly, almost dropping the ladle of hot dal, and looked at her in shock. That made two, with her and Devika asking her this question in one day!

Was it so transparent and obvious? Where did she go wrong in concealing her meetings with Sébastien? They had tried to be ultra-discreet.

'Hahaha ... What makes you think such a thing? I am a servant like you, and we don't mix with masters.'

'Sébastien is not a master, he is a worker just like you and me. The only difference is that he is white'

'You see, this is what I meant, whites and Indians cannot mix'

'Who told you so? Of course, they can be together if they are in love. So, are you and Sébastien together? Does Madame know?'

'*Chut* ... yes, he likes me' admitted Shanti, making a twisted coy smile.

'I knew it!' A shadow passed over her face. 'Look at me, are you serious? Do you know what it means?'

'Not so loud ...you'

'You have to tell me everything ....' A silence fell between them.

Veronique felt her heart shatter in hundred pieces. So, her instincts and fears were right. The only man she liked was taken by Shanti, a tea picker. No joy in life would be equal to that of having caught Sébastien for herself. Alas, that was not going to happen. He never reciprocated, despite all the attention and loving care she showed him from the very first day he arrived. She did not pursue him and accepted that fate had written Sébastien onto Shanti's palm lines.

'Very well then, I am going to refresh myself, change and take a painkiller' Veronique said as she dragged her tired feet on the cool polished floor, to disappear into her room.

26 BUN IN THE OVEN

'It's Holi tomorrow,' Devika said. 'You know, while playing with colours, men drink country liquor and *bhang*-laced sherbet? This festival lets us do all that. Even women cannot resist drinking *bhang* which was green cannabis leaves ground as a paste added to milk, flavoured with cardamom and sugar and boiled. This festival is different – the day you can smear the face of a woman with *gulal* and drink and beat the drum singing, right? Stay inside and don't open the door to anybody. You never know what pranks you may be subjected to.'

The next day, Shanti went directly to the greengrocer and bought a coconut, some incense sticks and small packets of *gulal* and *kumkum* powders. She went to the temple and gave everything to the priest, along with some money, saying that her offerings were for Lord Ram and Sita, the deities her mother always had worshipped. She sat cross-legged on the floor and listened quietly as the mantras were chanted. She was asking the gods to bless her and make Sébastien and her as a couple for life.

The ritual burning of the effigy of *Holika*, the demoness, signifying the victory of good over evil takes place in the night. With the sun going down in the west, men gathered around heaps of dry leaves, twigs and tree branches and started a bonfire.

The next morning when celebrations started, men, women and children came out on the street with colours, but she stayed in the villa; she did not trust herself to remain calm in the midst of Holi revelries. Shanti thought of Sébastien only, while a group came to the villa, playing drums and cymbals, singing jolly folk songs in Bhojpuri, everybody was throwing gulal powder or spraying each other with coloured water. Devika distributed some money and sweets and accepted a *tilak* of *kumkum*.

Shanti loved looking at the colours. Next year for Holi, she would wish to wear her *sindoor* and play as a married woman next to Sébastien, her *devta*. She had done all she could to protect him, offerings to the Gods, and mantras recited at the temple. It was now up to the gods to give him guidance on the matter. She was not sure that she would want to live if she ever lost the only other person, she had ever loved with all her heart.

Night fell, and the sounds of celebration in the nearby village began to fade. Sébastien came back home, parking the car in a screeching sound of the tyres on the gravel of the driveway. He went to look for Shanti in the kitchen. The young woman was startled to see him so openly coming to meet her. Veronique went about doing her tasks, pretending she was unfazed.

'Shanti, come with me a minute please,'

'Yes *Missier*'

'How many times have I asked you not to call me *Missier*? ... Sébastien, just Sébastien'

When they reached the corridor, he took her hand, 'Meet me tonight in the garden after everyone has dined and had their tea, retired to their rooms, I mean, you understand what I am trying to say?'

Shanti nodded quickly and dashed back to the kitchen. Veronique did not lift her eyes to look at her. It felt as if she did not want to betray her own countenance.

Shanti opened the door very softly, pulled it shut stealthily, and sneaked out towards the garden. She stood for a while in the shadows of the trees but could not see any signs of life. She thought that it was a good sign. That everyone had gone to sleep.

‘Shanti, Ma Cherie’

It thrilled her to hear his voice in the soft semi darkness of the night.

‘I am going to London and Paris on Monday. Devika has asked me to present the samples myself to the auctioneers. I will be away for a month, or maybe two. I need to visit my parents in Brittany too.’

‘Sébastien, how will I live not seeing you for so long? I am going to die. Hey Bhagwan!’

‘Don’t talk like that, you have everyone else at the house, and I shall write to you. My parents are old and not keeping very well. I miss them.’

‘Take me with you then’

‘No, *Ma Cherie*, I will be back soon. Perhaps we can find a house and live together.’

‘So, we are getting married ?!’ Shanti felt herself blushing, her heart leaping with joy. But the restrained tone of Sébastien cut her euphoria short.

'Marriage? no, not yet. But we can live together'

'We don't live together if we are not married. This is not the custom here.' Shanti shuddered in the night and asked to go back to the villa. Sébastien had just inched his way to an exit from her life. She felt nauseous at the unsettling reaction of his intention not to marry. After all, *Mawsi* might be right. White men and local workers like her never can have a future together.

Sébastien left quietly, early morning. The three women in the house looked at him with closed faces as he loaded the jeep. Each one having their own thoughts. Shanti carried on with her tasks the following days, often crying when no one was around her. Veronique could not muster her courage to either comfort her or let her suffer in silence. She took on more chores to keep herself occupied rather than watching the desolate Shanti slowly closing in on herself. Devika kept her head firmly balanced, having to rely upon her management of the estate and the forlorn faces of the two women. Sébastien surely had thrown some rocks in the mud when he arrived. She did not want to hear about anymore sad endings to a relationship. She was nursing her own with all the strength she had. The infatuation of Veronique had not escaped her noticing how the latter was holding her head high when she knew that Sébastien was courting Shanti.

The days seemed long after Sébastien left. Two women, each trying to bury their emotional misery behind chores, while Devika wonders what will become of her samples. She has put all her hopes for Bonne Espérance's future in Sébastien's hands.

*

The first letter arrived following a telegram. Sébastien did well at the auction. The tea samples were well received, and he was on the way to get a first order. He was leaving for Brittany next. He did not write to Shanti nor mention her in any of the missives. The young woman had a drawn face and was eating poorly. Veronique listened to her kind self and was looking after her. Shanti had been feeling sick a few times.

'I will make you some vegetable soup of pumpkin, celery, carrot, *mooli*, and some rice. It will soothe your stomach. Drink some ginger infusion afterwards, this will make your nausea go'.

Devika heard about Shanti being unwell and went to see her in her room. The curtains were drawn, and she found Shanti lying on the bed in a foetal position.

'Shanti, how are you feeling now?' The latter moved and tried to get up when she saw the mistress. She had dark circles under her eyes and looked quite unwell.

'I hear that you have not been eating well. Do you have any pain anywhere?'

'Non-Madame, I am alright, just a bit of an upset stomach.'

'Shall I ask the doctor to come? Are you still being sick?'

'Listen Shanti, if it is about Sébastien, you need not worry, he is coming back. He must be very busy traveling and working. So, no need to get yourself into such a state. All will be well. I promise you.'

As Devika was turning to go while lifting a reassuring hand on Shanti's shoulder, the young woman extended her hand to hold Devika's hand.

'Madame, there is something more .... I want to tell you'

Devika felt a lump in her throat. She was not ready to hear what her fear was telling her to believe had happened.

'Yes, don't worry, you can tell me anything. You are under my responsibility in this house.'

'Sit a minute Madame ...' said Shanti, smoothing the bed sheet next to her.

Devika sat down, taking Shanti's hand *into hers*. Looking into her eyes, she bid her to speak.

'I was not sure ... I wanted to tell Sébastien, but the two nights before he was leaving, he said he will not marry as yet.'

'Tell him what? Shanti'

'That I may be with child, I mean; *en voie de famille*.' Saying that, Shanti broke into tears. Devika gulped with a lump in her throat, after all, her instinct was right! What she did not want to hear, had happened. Love is such a devious thing. Under a good star, it is the most amazing thing to happen to someone, but its ramifications were always painful. Shanti is pregnant with Sébastien's child. What will she do now?

‘Don’t worry for now, get yourself better, we shall sort it out when Sébastien is back.’

Devika almost heard herself saying aloud what she was already rehearsing to say to Sébastien when he returned.

‘You should take Shanti to her relatives and marry her. It’s the only decent thing to do. You love the girl; you don’t have time for silly tea estate prejudices. The folks here are ready to ostracize this poor girl if she is rejected by you. Do the decent thing, embrace her, you have my full support.’ Things will be in order once again.

27 MARIE

Sébastien's father's health had deteriorated, but he was mentally alert. After a week spent meeting his relatives and his sister's new family, Sébastien began to go out alone. He was surprised how much Guerlesquin had changed during his absence. The corner Épicerie, where he had always shopped, had expanded under the new owners. The barber who had always cut his hair was dead. A few of his friends had moved away. There was much talk about the current state of affairs of the country in the village bar. He realized how much he had missed relationships and conversations that did not revolve around tea. He had almost forgotten the joys of the local theatre. Now, he had the chance to indulge in these pleasures once again. New words had crept into his vocabulary, and the accent from his family sounded almost new to him. The French summer felt mild after the heat and humidity he had got used to. The rain seemed gentle after the heavy downpours of some of the Mauritian cyclones.

Life on the plantation was hard, and he was always busy. The only music he heard there was played on the gramophone, apart from the wireless radio which picked up transmissions from the national stations which ran concurrently in French and English with interludes of Hindi songs. Sébastien smiled at the thought of returning to Bonne Espérance. Folks at the clubs with their wives would come over to listen to the new records he would take with him. Paul would expect a good Gauloise puff, he so often talked about, and the Gruyère cheese. Ignoring that there were better Breton ones with their red labels of AOC. These did not reach the island, so his ignorance was excused.

Sébastien saw Marie, his sister's friend and the girl next door, on the bus. In a gesture of friendliness, he went up to her and struck up a conversation. The picture of the two girls giggling together flashed through his mind. He was thrilled when he discovered Marie still remembered him. She was delighted to see him after so many years.

'I thought you would return home much sooner than this! I kept pestering your parents for news about you.'

To say that he was flattered was an understatement. Marie had turned into a beautiful woman. They got off at the same stop and walked home together. Sébastien walked her home. Before they parted outside her house, she kissed his cheek and said, 'Goodnight, Seb. It was lovely seeing you again.'

'I am here for another five months,' Sébastien heard himself lie, hiding his surprise at the sudden familiarity that had sprung between them.

'I am sure we'll be seeing more of each other.'

'I hope so,' she replied breathlessly. Before he could turn and walk away, she added, 'I've missed you.' Sébastien thought of their easy conversation on the bus. It was the first time during his stay that he had not felt like a stranger, an outsider in his hometown.

The next evening, he went to her home and invited her to the port for a drink and a stroll. The pink flush on her cheeks... was it only his imagination? She suggested that they go early in the day, because she wanted to visit an art gallery that was exhibiting the work of a new artist. They went to a classy French restaurant for a meal, where soft music and good wine flowed in abundance.

The girl sitting in front of him was beautiful,

dressed in a chic white linen dress, bright Carmine lipstick contrasting with her flawless pale skin, two tiny pearl studs as earrings, a faint perfume lingering in the air about her; everything felt like a dream. Even the waiter, who wheeled a cart laden with a variety of cheeses after the meal, seemed to have stepped out of a world Sébastien had long forgotten about. Too much time had passed since he sat across a small table from a charming woman in the anonymous privacy of a restaurant. The closeness that verged on intimacy was exhilarating and romantic. He had missed this kind of life for a very long time. Meals for him back on the island were at either the house or the club. Busy on the tea estate, he had never thought this life could be his again.

'How come such a beautiful woman like you is still single?'

Marie blinked in surprise.

'Have you forgotten that you asked me to wait

for you? Didn't your parents tell you that I always asked them about you?'

Sébastien was taken aback. Neither his parents, nor he, had thought that her questions held anything more than a natural interest to know more about a childhood friend. He frantically searched his memory for any words he had spoken that might have been mistaken for a promise. He found none. He remembered her as the childhood friend of his sister who always came to their house. They had parties with the others, danced, drank, went to the beach for swimming, fishing, and he remembered they kissed too. But a promise?

'That was years ago. We were children,' he tried to wave it off.

'You didn't mean it?!' Marie's eyes widened with surprise. He imagined he saw a flicker of disappointment in them. Was the shine in her eyes caused by tears' swelling? It was incredible that a woman so young and attractive would have carried a torch for him all these years.

'*Non* ... hmm. I was serious at the time,' he immediately caught himself lying for the second time. 'Still, we were only children. I was about 15 or 16 then'. He could not bring himself to correct her assumption and embarrass her.

'You were not that young, not to understand my feelings, Sébastien'

There was reproach in her voice. She leaned forward and asked, 'Is there some exotic beauty you have met on that faraway island, Sébastien?'

'I'm not married, you can see.' He placed his ring-less hands on the table, one on each side of the narrow white vase that held two pink roses. His heart thumped thinking about Shanti. He was betraying her so easily. Yet, he felt guilt free. A new him was uncovering himself. He lied, flirted, while Shanti was waiting for him. Was it the fact that he was comfortably at home, quite free?

He took a sip of wine before he spoke again. 'I'll never leave my life as a tea estate manager. I love it too much. I've not missed Guerlesquin when I was there, as much as I miss the gardens when I'm here. I've only been home for a month, yet I long for the gong that calls the tea pickers to work or tells them when they have time off. I miss the quiet, the forest birds, the heat, the rain, even some of the damned insects. Still, it is not a life I could ask a girl like you to share. You live a protected life here, and over there, things might be too extreme for you. Then, there are other things to consider as well.'

'Tell me about them and let me be the judge.' Marie reached across the table and laid her hand over his.

'What other things?'.

Marie's touch was soft which excited him. He turned his hand over and held hers. He looked down at the oval nails that had been neatly painted to match her lipstick. Suddenly, the memory of Shanti's work-roughened hands with broken nails no nail polish had ever touched, came to him with startling clarity. The hard skin between her fingers – the trademark of tea pickers – had softened, but the corns under her skin would never disappear.

Shanti still loves me.

She has given up everything, including her reputation, just to be with me and to make me happy. What am I doing here holding another woman's hand? Sébastien looked at Marie's hand and considered disentangling his fingers from hers.

But then, why shouldn't I? What do I owe her? Many white managers have had a local woman for years only to marry a girl from their own country. Seems like Marie loves me. She has never thought another man was right for her. I've never written to her, and yet, she has waited. He must decide.

Well, he never made Shanti any promises. He never said he would marry her. It had been a wonderful interlude, but it was clearly time for him to return to reality, to the mainstream. At the end of the day, he wanted a home with a French woman beside him to grow old with. He wanted to nod off to sleep in a rocking chair in front of a French fireplace, with a newspaper in his hand, his glasses on his nose and a glass of Calvados next to him. Right now, his mind was playing up, or was it the wine? When he had rum at Bonne Espérance, he felt like wanting to be close to Shanti. Certainly, his alcohol intake could be blamed.

'What are you thinking about? You have a queer smile on your face,' Marie pressed his hand. She was smiling now. He looked at her, relieved that she could not see that another woman was inhabiting the space they were in.

'It sounds so perfect! Now describe a scene from these tea gardens you speak so passionately about.'

Sébastien spent a couple of minutes thinking of a suitable answer.

'What can I say? I shall try ....it is evening, and it has just stopped raining. The air hangs around a deep smell of Petrichor. A unique scent following a rain shower – when the world seems to sigh with pleasure, and people unconsciously perhaps, breathe in a little more deeply, savouring the scents in return.

During the early rains, which is also called the cyclonic season, you can hear the stream that passes the estate right up the villa. It can swell 10 times its normal size, and it will roar with the fast flow. An unshaded electric bulb lights up the veranda, but you can hardly see the bulb, because night insects are swarming around it. The sound of frogs is mingled with the cicadas, loud enough to make sleep difficult.

Sometimes, a rat squeaks and you know that they are having their diner. Grey house lizards and bright green Geckos are upon the ceilings of the veranda, feasting on the insects. Their tongues flick out and then back again, too fast to be seen. If you listen closely, you can hear a soft pop each time an insect's head is crushed in their mouths. The floor is covered with small, gauzy wings. Giant African snails slide their way leaving their slimy trails on the floor and join the feast. The air now cooled after the shower; makes you wonder whether the moths have got to your woollens. For there are holes in them despite the naphthalene balls that Veronique puts in the wardrobe. Veronique is the house help. This helps prevent mildew that grows on every moist surface – your clothes and shoes included. Your cigarettes and matches are kept beside the light too. It keeps the tobacco from getting soggy.'

'That's so beautiful, I can believe how you can't think of living here anymore, it sounds like a slice of paradise out there.'

'Yes, I believe it is. Do you think you can live

the kind of life I've just talked about, Marie? Think well before you answer.'

Sébastien was imagining how his life could be with a French wife on an exotic island. He would be able to have long conversations with someone who knows his culture and relate to his day to day happenings. So far, he could only meet Shanti to spend some time with her but his thirst for a long conversation on Molière, cheese, wine or just any topic that interested him were left barren. Apart from the tea world that surrounded Shanti, her knowledge of the world was shrouded in long years of being unexposed to the outside world.

Marie looked at his face, searching for a sign that this was an elaborate joke.

'Are you asking me to go there, and live there with you?' She sounded excited and happy; her face lit up with a smile.

'Umm... take it like this'

'Sébastien, are you proposing marriage to me?'

'Well, it certainly looks like I am... But can you say it's too sudden?' Sébastien laughed.

He had just surprised himself with his own impulsiveness. He had not expected a proposal to be the outcome of what he had thought would be a pleasant evening in the town with an old friend. It may have been the nostalgic trip down memory lane, the wine, the soft music, or even Marie's intoxicating perfume. It smelled like Chanel, and as Coco said, 'a girl wearing Chanel must be classy and fabulous'. Marie was both.

The thought that she had loved him all these years filled him with a sense of dignity and self-respect, the qualities that his tea managers friends said he had lost when he took up with a local woman.

Marie would keep a fine home and create the atmosphere that he had so missed. She would make sure that the walls had elegant art adorning them, the air had faint and tasteful music in the evenings, and of course, the homey ambience was not complete without beautifully arranged fresh cut flowers in every room. With her, he could talk about anything, life in France, friends that they had in common, or other things that interested them both. Her sense of fashion and her graceful gait would make him the envy of all the other people.

Yes, she would certainly outshine every other woman on the tea estate. With her on his arm, he could rise one step above the other men. He firmly pushed away the last remnants of thoughts about Shanti. France was home, and where he would eventually be buried, and he must take this sense of belonging with him no matter which corner of the world he went to. His father had also asked him to get married soon, as he would like to see his bride before he died. The poor man did not look as if he would last long. All these thoughts made perfect sense to Sébastien. What he was deciding on the instant was the solution to everything.

'What is your answer?' He looked up at her expectantly.

Marie's slow smile said it all, even before she voiced it out loud.

'That is so sudden, and unexpected. what can I say?'

'Say yes ... you waited for me long enough, didn't you?'

A beaming Marie gave an affirmative nod, looking into his eyes.

'Thank you for making me a happy man Marie. I'll try to be a good husband,' he said and kissed her hand.

Sébastien sealed his fate with an instant decision. This marriage would mean the end of his 'illegitimate and disgraceful' affair with Shanti, as Paul had put it.

Marie set the date and they both went to see

the priest for the earliest day available for the church ceremony. The wedding was in the *salle des fêtes* and both their families were in attendance with all their friends. Sébastien's father could not stop smiling and sat watching the radiant couple dance and kiss. He felt relieved, now that his son was settled, had a wife. He could travel and work in this distant island, he would no longer be worried about him. He knew they would be both happy together.

28 MARRIED LIFE

The long journey by ship and train had done nothing to dampen Marie's enthusiasm. She was ready to discover this little paradise as Sébastien called it. When the car arrived at the villa, Marcel called out loudly to say that Sébastien had arrived.

Shanti watched the man she already considered as her husband come out of the car. She controlled her desire to run to him. He had been absent for much longer than the promised month. Sebastien's face did not have its usual smile, he did not even look around for her. His walk was stiff as he turned to open the other passenger door. Shanti squeezed the hem of her blouse, waiting in anticipation with a strange feeling of dread.

A tall blonde woman emerged, dressed in a beige linen suit with matching handbag and shoes. She looked around her, then at the villa, saw Shanti standing on the steps of the veranda, and smiled at her.

Sébastien followed the direction of her gaze and met with Shanti's eyes. Then, Shanti caught the gleam of the gold band on the third finger of his left hand. She closed her eyes, reeling from the knowledge of what had happened in France. Her relationship with Sébastien was over. She was warned by the women in the village "The moment the masters cross the sea, they forget everything," She had foolishly put it all down to prejudice or jealousy. Now, she felt as if she had received a fist in her stomach. They were so right!

Shanti stepped aside to let the new couple pass

her in the doorway, with a slight bowing of her head. Her eyes were streaming with tears. She didn't know whether she could hear her heart break or a hissing in her ears, telling her to disappear on the spot. She felt like Sita when Ram had doubted her chastity, and she had cried for her Mother to take her back. The earth had split open and swallowed her. This is how Shanti felt. Looking at the new wife and her happy face was a harsh reminder of her present humiliation and rejection. Not a word from him, and now he walks in ... married. He did not even bother to greet her. Shanti touched her belly feeling ashamed in front of her unborn child.

Veronique came to welcome the couple with a look of astonishment on her face, looking at Marie. She also had lost her voice. And barely responded to the greeting of both Sébastien and his wife.

After some time, Sébastien came to the kitchen. He watched Shanti pump the primus stove. She struck a match and set fire to the thin jet of kerosene.

'I'm sorry,' he finally said. 'I had not intended it, I swear. But Marie has always loved me, and I need a family I can spend my old age in my own country.' Shanti ladled water from a large jar into an enamel kettle. She placed the kettle carefully on the stove before she spoke.

'I knew this would happen someday, *Missier*. I should be grateful for the time we have had together. It was as beautiful as it was short-lived. I borrowed you for a while from your real wife, the wife who had still not come into your life. I took my happiness when I found it and have paid for it in instalments. I was already an orphan, losing my parents. Now, I have lost you as well. I have been trying to prepare myself for my loss, since our first night together. I have no complaints against you.' She took a deep breath.

'My only request is that you do something for

our child'

'Our child .... what do you mean?!'

'You promised you would write to me. So, I was waiting to tell you. I am pregnant.' Sébastien was speechless. His face went pale. His eyes widened in disbelief. He just walked in with his new wife, and hears that Shanti is bearing his child.

'Have your tea and leave, *Missier* Sébastien. Your wife must be expecting you.'

She turned to arrange a few homemade biscuits on a plate. She placed two cups and saucers on a tray and carried it to the table. He watched her arrange the table. He looked for tears. He even hoped for some, but there were none. Shanti returned with the tray and did not send another glance his way. Sébastien realized he still loved Shanti.

His heart always would; Marie was his mind's choice, but Shanti .... This woman had put him above everything else in her life.

By serving him so well, she had forgotten who she was, and lost herself to him. Marie and he had the same upbringing, spoke the same language, laughed at the same jokes, and moved in the same social circles. She was the woman he wanted to be seen with. Shanti catered to his every whim, gave in to his every desire, while Marie challenged his intellect.

The thought that Shanti was pregnant with his child made him feel distressed. He needed legitimate children. He looked at Shanti. He did not have to explain.

She was watching him now, the look on her face said it all –she understood.

He knew that Shanti was hurting, and yet, he could do nothing to comfort her. He felt helpless and blamed himself for not being able to be there for her. Yet, when he was in Brittany, he felt he could forget Shanti and was ready to embrace his life with Marie by his side.

Now, he was feeling guilty. With a sense that he had committed a huge mistake. A child with it, his world came crashing down, unexpectedly.

*

Despite everything Sébastien had told Marie about the weather, it came as an unwelcome surprise to her. She had never experienced such high temperatures before, even on the hottest Summers in Brittany, the Atlantic breeze cooled the land quickly.

The electricity went out several times during the day. Without electricity, the fans would not work, and there was no way to cool off. She spent this time on the veranda, leaning against the stout wooden railing, trying to catch the slightest breeze. The mountains in the distance became hazy, shadows became fuzzy patches on the ground, the plants wilted, and birdsong stopped. Hens sat with their wings away from their bodies and their beaks open. Even the golden sunlight of kinder seasons began to seem harsh, almost metallic. There was a strange stillness and quietness. The first cool breeze brought immediate change. Smiles reappeared.

Marie ventured out to the vegetable garden at some distance from the house. She held her skirt down with both hands against the naughty wind which had picked up suddenly. A gardener was turning the soil over with a small hoe, looked over his shoulder to the hills and said, 'Go home quickly, Madame. It is going to rain.' It was Marcel.

'I've seen rain before,' she smiled. She was wrong. This was nothing like the sweet rain in Brittany that touched the shoulder like a loving friend.

The clouds approached very rapidly, like a great black wall. The big raindrops hit her with a force that made her think of peas from a peashooter. Big drops splat on any surface they reached. Only Wintry gales brought heavy rains in Guerlesquin, but nothing so sudden, with such force.

She was fully drenched before turning to go back and reach the veranda. The rainy season had just begun, with anticyclones looming around often. It rained for a week without letting up. She remained cooped up inside the house, waiting for the sun to come out. She read every book she could find in her bedroom. As Sébastien was always busy, he'd be away from home for long hours, she had to find ways to kill time.

The only vegetables cooked in the house were ones she had never tasted before but was getting used to. Steak or ham were not on the menu. Both Veronique and Shanti barely spoke to her. They only served her what she asked for and replied politely to any question she asked. She had met Devika a few times, she had been warm and cordial, but without advancing any more branches of friendship. Life on the tea estate was proving more daunting than Marie imagined. Sébastien was most often aloof, or tired from work. Their romantic moments had come to a halt. It started to bother Marie. Where is the paradise?

*

Devika went to Shanti's room one afternoon, when the house was quiet, and everyone seemed to be taking a rest. She knocked gently at the door. Shanti came to open. She had a drawn face, dark circles around her large almond shaped eyes.

'May I come in?

'Please Madame, of course' Shanti tried to draw a faint smile while allowing Devika to pass by the door. Her room was spotless, and she had a small altar by the window where a terracotta lamp was lit in front of a framed picture of a Durga Ma. A glass of water served as a vase where a couple of fresh flowers from the garden looked like spots of red and yellow.

'Shanti I need to ask you something if you don't mind' said Devika, feeling very emotional to see her in this state. The latter nodded but said nothing, keeping her eyes lowered.

'Sébastien has come back with a wife. He did not even tell me he was getting married. Now that you are with a child, what are you going to do? Have you thought about it? did you have time to talk to him?'

Shanti sobbed convulsively, and Devika had to comfort her. She didn't want to evoke such a question knowing her state of mind already, but the matter had to be addressed as soon as possible. The young girl had no one who could support her apart from Devika herself. Her soreness from being abandoned in her pregnant state by her husband was more than enough for her to feel what Shanti must be going through. She has had the good fortune of a miracle in the form of Bonne Espérance coming to her. Shanti had nothing. She stood all the chance of being ostracized by her relatives and shunned by the whole village.

After a few minutes of awkward silence, Shanti wiped her tears and looked at Devika, recomposing herself.

'Madame, *Missier* ... my *devta* left me for another woman. I was too lowly for him to consider marrying me. Now God has blessed me with his child, it will be born without a father recognising him or her. What do I do? Tell me yourself...'

The agony and despair of the young woman cut the air thin, making it almost unbreathable.

'You can always stay here; you know that I will support and look after your welfare. Veronique is a good friend too, and her kindness knows no bounds. However, I am thinking it might become a torture for you to bear the presence of Marie with Sébastien. Can you go to your home until the baby is born?'

'My *Mawsi's* home? .... in my state! She told me

that I should consider the nearby river to throw myself in, when I told her about Sébastien and me, and now pregnant out of wedlock? I might as well be dead before I show my face to her'

'Oh, I am so sorry my poor girl, there must be a solution to your situation. But don't get me wrong. You are here in what you can consider your own house now, we shall sort you out. Now rest and have something to eat later. You need to think of your baby now. You need to feed for two, all that matters are that you keep yourself healthy and strong for your baby.'

Devika left Shanti to calm down. She had found herself in such a situation before and felt as if she was going mad.

Sébastien came to seek a conversation with Devika the next morning. He waited till Marie had gone into her room and no one was around in the dining hall. Devika had taken her place on the rattan chair on the veranda and getting her notes ready for some more sketches. This had become her favourite place in the house, where she was sheltered but could feel the outdoor surrounding her at all times.

'Devika, do you have a moment?'

'Of course, is everything alright?'

Yes, and no. Marie is trying to adapt to her new life. The problem is Shanti.' Devika gave him a stern look, waiting for his next words. Sébastien felt the tension, he had not slept well, and needed to talk about his torment to someone neutral. In this vast estate, there was no one he could confide in. Paul would either damn him to hell or push him to do what he would hate doing. Devika was his only chance. Her calmness and wise self-had often impressed him.

'Shanti and I were in a relationship. But ...umm. I never ever promised her marriage. She got herself pregnant without my consent. Now that I am married, I fear that my wife will know, and this will destroy our lives. I can't trust anyone enough to tell this, that's why I have come to you for advice.'

'I see, you were in a relationship, but you were not serious about her. Did you know that she could not have a future once she's been with a man? In this country, things are still difficult when it comes to such traditions. Prejudices pile in heaps. The poor girl is an orphan and her relatives would not concede into either supporting her or accept her current state. What are you going to do?'

'I am not sure, but I cannot recognize the child when it is born. If this is what Shanti wants. I am now a married man. What will I tell Marie?'

'Did you talk to Shanti?'

'I did, the same day I arrived. She has asked me to do something for our child. Apart from money, what else can I provide her with?'

'You have a strange way of showing it,' Devika said. 'You were ready to sacrifice her happiness for yours, only to keep the social privileges that you will lose if you did the right thing by her.'

'I am ashamed to have put Shanti in this position, but we had a talk before I left, and I was clear that marriage was not in the equation. And I was shocked to hear the news when I arrived.'

'So, your relationship with her, as you say it, all the time has been for amusement only? Sorry, it's none of my business but there is protection these days... Sébastien! If she couldn't for many obvious reasons, you could have taken your responsibility. Now, it's two lives wrecked.'

Sébastien turned his face away, he realised that this conversation was not going anywhere except to highlight his wrongdoing. Devika had aligned with Shanti. It was understandable.

'I will talk to Shanti. It will be better for you not to further her agony. Stay away from her before this house witnesses another drama, if your wife comes to know about it. That will break three hearts at one go, if I may count yours as part of it, can I?' She plastered a smile on her face and continued the conversation, though deep inside, she felt truly sickened. This man was only worried about his own situation, not that of Shanti, nor what would happen to their unborn child. This reminded her of her own husband who had not shown any sign to know about his own child. She could not comprehend men.

'Yes, ...yes' Sébastien's gaze was fixed on a corner of the coffee table. He got up and left.

Devika felt upset and tried to concentrate on her work as a diversion. She needed to speak to Shanti about a plan that was slowly hatching in her head.

Veronique came to bring her some lemon tea and some samosas. She had an inquisitive look on her face. As if she also needed to know about what Shanti will do. Devika got up after another hour of work and got dressed. She asked Marcel to take her to the neighbouring town. There, to go down in front of a chapel, on a side road, next to a flat expanse of vegetable gardens. There was a concrete building behind the chapel, painted in white. A nun came to open the door to the office next to the entrance. Devika stayed in for some time, enough for Marcel to smoke two cigarettes while waiting under a java apple tree full of delicate pink fruits. Devika left shortly with renewed strength.

She decided to talk to Shanti that evening. The young woman looked like she had got back her composure and was out in the kitchen helping making dinner.

'Shanti, can I talk to you later?'

'Yes, Madame, after dinner and tidying the kitchen, I will come to your room, is it alright?'

She was no longer comfortable to sit under the veranda after dinner, where Marie and Sébastien had started enjoying the falling night, retiring late to their room.

'Shanti, I went to see Sister Claire today. She runs a shelter for young women, who need support when they have nowhere to go facing various social issues. She has agreed to give you a room there. You can stay till your baby is born. I will bear all the extra expenses and you will continue getting your salary. Maybe you have a friend or relative you can trust who can visit you and whom you want when the delivery time comes. But, if it is difficult, Veronique and I will always be here for you.'

Shanti joined her hands together near her heart in a Namaste and bowed her head, with tears rolling down her cheeks.

'Madame I am truly blessed to have met you. I will be forever grateful for your kind help. I can ask my childhood friend Mintah to visit from time to time.'

'Very well then, done! Get your things ready to pack, we shall get Marcel to drop you when you are ready.'

'I shall be ready to go next Monday.'

29 DELIVERY

Sister Claire had granted Shanti the permission to set up something that could keep her busy during the months before her baby was born. She opened a small shop in the rooms that had a separate entrance at the side of the chapel away from the main door. She sold clothes sewed by herself and other women of the shelter. Veronique did a bit too and brought them when she visited Shanti.

She put up shelves and stocked them with embroidery, handmade toys, and knitted garments. The business was small, but it kept her busy. Mintah sometimes came over to help her make jams, pickles, and *mazavaroo*. She dried bilimbi and mango in the sun, lightly coated them with oil, and stored them in large jars. They sold well during winter, when few fresh vegetables came to the market. It was hard work and Shanti earned little, but she ignored her aching muscles, discomfort of her growing belly and kept trying to keep her mind of other distractions. Devika was already paying for her expenses at the shelter; she did not wish to become one of her financial burdens.

*

Sago palms and ferns and flowering tropical plants grew in giant pots, in the rooms, on the veranda, lining the steps that led down to the lawn where Devika took her afternoon tea. Once a week, a dhobi came to take the household linen away to be laundered. Life went on after Shanti left for the shelter without anyone asking about her. Which was for the best. Veronique visited her on Sunday afternoons, bringing her little treats she had made. If Sébastien noticed the absence of Shanti, he made sure he did not ask for her whereabouts. Conveniently, so. He understood that Devika had made some arrangements to avoid any clash in the house.

Marie accompanied her husband to various social events. She found the conversations at the planters' club difficult to follow, with the technical, botanical, and agricultural jargon. Sometimes, she asked the person next to her to explain, and sometimes, she made a mental note of the words and asked Sébastien about them later. He enjoyed all the socializing at first, but soon, he began to miss his quiet life. Marie was trying too hard to fit in, to make him happy, and he appreciated that, but there were times when he just wanted to sleep. He did not enjoy feeling obliged to take his wife somewhere because she had been alone all day.

Marie thought that a baby would be the answer to her loneliness, but she could feel no pleasure when she soon became pregnant. She was constantly unwell, nausea wracking her stomach endlessly. Sébastien tried to be sympathetic, but he believed she was fussing too much. He had not witnessed Shanti's first trimester and didn't know whether she also was in such a miserable state. When he saw her in her fifth month, she had never complained of headache or a loss of appetite. She had not demanded anything special. She went about her chores as usual. It was probably unfair to compare the two women, but he could not help it.

Marie gave up tennis for fear of a miscarriage. There were many things she wanted to say, but she quietly complied. She embroidered her initials on the bed linen and her handkerchiefs. She joined Devika's company on the veranda, and tried her hand at painting, but her attempts ended in frustration. She knew enough about art to realize that her pictures were too studied and her use of colour, uninspired. Shadow and light did not mingle or highlight the subject the way it did in great paintings. Devika never offered a negative criticism when asked to appreciate her artwork. She knew the young woman was trying her best to keep busy.

It became increasingly difficult for Marie to present a cheerful face to Sébastien. She could not enjoy sitting in the club eating cucumber sandwiches and sipping lemonade, while the men indulged in different kinds of sporting activities.

The more engrossed she became with her condition, the more Sébastien's irritation grew. They either spent time together in silence or an argument. Eventually, she decided to go to Brittany for the birth. Sébastien did not oppose the idea, and happily sent her to France.

*

'I am not sure if God really exists,' Shanti said to Veronique during one of her visits. 'He seems to be something priests have created to make their own lives easier. If God were real, would He truly need the bother of prayers and rituals the priests conduct? Wouldn't He be fair to all the creatures He created?' 'Worshipping pictures and idols are silly, too' she said.

'Who was the first to make an image? The Bible does not mention any one person in particular. It was a general practice in the old days. God took up mud and made the first man in His own image, didn't He?' Is it not taught that Jesus asked his followers to be perfect, because he was so perfect? I take that to mean that I should try and be like him.'

'Why are you questioning God so much?' teased Veronique. Does Sister Claire drown you too much in sermons?'

'No, I just have enough time to reflect when I visit the chapel. I have always been a believer and have completely trusted God. Why am I in this situation today? It seems as if a curse is persisting since my own birth. My mother also fell in love with a white man, who left her after she became pregnant.'

Shanti had felt many times that she should not have been born. Her birth made her mother's life miserable that she didn't live after giving birth to her. What will become of her now after she gives birth to her own baby? Was this sorrow of abandonment perpetuating in time?

Cold winter winds blew down from the mountains, giving jolts of fear to Shanti who cradled her enormous belly with apprehension. Some evenings, the coldness almost overpowered her, and the extra blankets given by Sister Claire were not warm enough for her. Her teeth would chatter, feeling almost numb in her feet; she was grateful for Veronique's old sweater and the extra fleece blanket Devika had given her. With the kicks and movement of the baby, Shanti got excited. She missed Sébastien terribly. She felt lonely but was grateful for all the support Devika and Veronique gave her.

*

When the midwife was called by Sister Claire, Shanti was in the throes of pain of childbirth. The woman came fully kitted with towels, oil, linen, and other paraphernalia in a huge raffia bag. She lit incense and loban in a small darkened burner, black from overuse. She was fully in charge and made sure that the smoke would drive evil spirits away. According to her, it was important to drive away any bad energy so that the delivery goes smoothly.

When the baby arrived, she would burn some more, to ensure his safety. As a calm and collected midwife who knew what she was doing, she remained unfazed by Shanti's screams. The latter suffered terrible labour pains that went on for hours. She pushed and panted until her strength nearly failed. Her screams kept everyone on edge throughout the night. With each composed move, she helped Shanti gain confidence and push to deliver her baby.

A boy was born. The new mother turned her face to the wall to hide her tears. The midwife had seen the same sinking feeling in the eyes of every mother clutching her baby, the same shock and joy of seeing what she carried for nine months. She picked up the new-born and placed her on Shanti's chest. However, when the latter held her baby in her arms for the first time, she did not hold back tears of disappointment. She had always been told how beautiful babies were. No one had prepared her for a new born baby who looked old and wrinkled; with blurry eyes and a nose so bulbous, it looked like a red onion. "A boy, and an ugly one," she whispered to herself

"Come, come, stop your tears. It will affect your milk. You will pass your distress onto the baby. You are just being silly. It's a new born baby, give yourself time.'

The midwife stroked Shanti's head as she continued, "The baby is beautiful; just wait and see. In a couple of weeks, you will see things completely differently. See how his little fingers clutch and hold onto yours. Have you thought of a name for him?"

Shanti's heart overflowed with protective love, which, she hoped, enveloped her baby. The feeling was so intense it almost hurt. She surrendered to the emotion and felt her dismay vanish almost instantly. Shanti kissed the baby and held him close to her face. Tears of joy filled her eyes, but she willed them away. Crying would be inauspicious. She pressed her lips against the baby's forehead and looked out of the window. A patch of pink sky with a silvery half-moon swam into her vision through the leftover tears.

'Nishant,' she whispered to the child.' 'You are my Nishant, my Moon, my pleasant early morning; my end of the night to a new day'.

"Now, that's a lovely name, Shanti."

The baby was not like his mother who had turned golden dusky as a tea picker under the constant sunshine. His eyes looked bluish and his wrinkly baby skin was rosy, and his hair was of a light golden brown. Shanti recognized all the bits of Sébastien in him. Sister Claire read some prayers over the new born and touched its forehead with her silver rosary.

'What a beautiful baby you have Shanti, Praise be the Lord!' Shanti smiled, thanking her before closing her eyes to rest from her exhaustion.

Devika and Marie, upon hearing the news, left everything they were doing and rushed to see Shanti and her baby. Devika brought many baby gifts, among her own daughter's, Beti's baby clothes. Veronique went outside to call Marcel to come in and see the baby. She was so excited, forgetting that no one except herself and Devika knew that Shanti was expecting when she arrived at the shelter. A very surprised Marcel hesitantly held the baby, with moist eyes. It all suddenly dawned to him why there were so many to and fro visits to the shelter.

'You have a beautiful baby, Shanti!' Gushed the old man.

'Where is the father?' All the three women stopped and exchanged glances.

Devika was going to say something, when Marcel shook his head and said, 'Don't say anything, I think I have my reasons to believe who it can be'.

Veronique smiled and looked at Devika, 'I was wondering Madame, shouldn't Shanti and the baby come back to the villa now? I could look after them, besides Shanti needs help with the baby before she is fit to be on her feet again.'

'You are always very kind Vero, bless you. Yes, I am thinking of that too. But how do we explain the baby to the world?'

'What's happened has happened, Madame. What more can she do now? She cannot conceal the baby from the world for the rest of her life. To hell with the world! They both deserve their place under the sun.' Veronique lowered her eyes for that excess of emotions.

'You are forgetting that Sébastien still lives in the house with us. Will this not be an uncomfortable situation?'

'Did he bother before? Why should we?'

'You are perhaps right. Better sooner than later. Living with heads held high is perhaps the best way. After all, Shanti has not committed any sin. So, why don't we help Shanti pack and let's go home!'

Shanti was feeding Nishant and smiled when she heard the word home.

*

It was a car full of happy heads that Marcel drove to the villa. He kept looking at the backseat where Shanti sat, holding her baby close to her. He smiled throughout the way. Devika was the best human Bonne Espérance could ever have had. Spreading her love, compassion and kindness to anyone who came to her. The tea estate of good hope could not have better deserved its name more than that. It was good that Shanti can stand on her feet, face the world and bring up her son with peace and happiness.

Baby Nishant arrived at Bonne Espérance in a soft blue woolly blanket with matching hat and socks. Sébastien was not home, and thankfully, Marie was away too. Both mother and child settled in Shanti's bedroom where Devika had a baby cot set up.

Shanti had not even sent a message to *Mawsi* that she has a son now. Probably, it was best avoided. The baby stirred, and Shanti moved to change his nappy. Her life as a young single mother had just begun.

30 RECONCILIATION

The colours that fall across the landscape of this remote highland corner of Mauritius are hewn from a different light. The eternal blue of the sky over the verdant hills sweep up to meet mountains afloat on a sea of clouds, skimming the edges of the shallow valley clefts, not far from Black River gorges, thick with wild green jungle.

The early mists linger, where, for a while, it is impossible to tell where the land ends and the sky begins. An eerie silence settles in, with the heavy moistness that hangs on the air, dampening the skin, raising the hairs on the arms in a light *frisson*. The sun is slow to rise and cast its unhurried warmth upon the ground, sweeping away the fragile dew, revealing the colourful saris of the tea pickers on their way along the flat terraces. Soon, their baskets slung behind their heads, would fill with the leaves prized for their healing properties, now cultivated as the compulsory drink on the island.

As far as the eye could see, emerald tea gardens clung to the hillsides, mile upon mile of undulating curves, hugging the steep slopes like moss on an aged stone, paths zigzagging through the low-slung shrubs, cushioning the landscape in miniature green clouds, arid silver trunks reaching gnarled tentacles down into the hardened ground.

Shanti was taking in the lush surroundings, standing on the steps from the veranda, a light shawl across her shoulders. She has missed this landscape she grew up with. At the shelter, there were no such views, to watch from the narrow windows. She heard quick steps behind her, which resonated on the polished timber floor. She recognised them. Her heart leapt with a thud.

“Shanti ....? An awkward silence hung in the air, while a bulbul sang on the nearby tamarind tree. Shanti did not turn to look at Sébastien. The man advanced closer. She could smell his aftershave.

‘How are you? I have not seen you for a long time, where have you been?’

‘Am alright *Missier*, just went away for a while.’

‘Alright, but you did not tell me.’ He looked at her postpartum belly, which was still round, it made her look like she was six months pregnant. He was confused. If his calculations were right, she should already have had the baby. But then, Sébastien did not know about the effects of postpartum. He did not believe what Shanti just told him. Knowing how the folks are here, her *Mawsi* could not have welcomed her with her baby.

'Away, where? Where is the baby?'

Shanti felt dizzy. What she had dreaded the most, is when Sébastien would talk to her, and mention their baby. She knew from the day he first held her hand in his, that she was doomed into heartbreak. It would come so fast, and with a baby in tow, was way beyond her expectations. What was there left to say anymore? When she saw his wedding ring, her world had come crashing down. She had been since engulfed in a cyclone of emotions. But suddenly, after the birth of her child, everything seemed calm. For once, and now he is here asking her such questions. How insensitive of him!

Shanti turned to look at Sebastien for the first time in months. He had taken a deeper tan, making his blue eyes glow more intensely, he had crow lines which she had never noticed earlier. He was still unabashedly handsome, like a god, her *Devta*. One who abandoned her to wrap his hand into another woman's hand

and bring her home as a wife. While she, Shanti remained the outcast.

'My baby? Umm... he is Nishant, my son' she muttered.

'We have a son?! Our child, and you didn't tell me?'

Shanti lifted her tired large brown eyes to look at Sébastien. Did she see a glimpse of hope there? Was he going to acknowledge their child despite being married to Marie?

'I had to get away from you and Madame Marie, and the others. People don't take kindly to a woman who gets pregnant out of wedlock. I had told you that *Missier* Sebastien. You never showed any interest or concern for me, as far as I remember.'

'Shanti, I am awfully guilty and ashamed of all the pain I've caused you. I was afraid of losing Marie.'

'Oh, I see, afraid of losing Marie ... and not of

losing me and your child?'

'No, this is not what I meant. I had persuaded Marie to come to Mauritius, because I felt I needed someone whom I could share everything that's familiar. I am excluded, but not sure you can understand what I mean, but it is true. I am not a white landowner here. I am French, and still a stranger to the land. You have given me everything, but I felt different when I went back home. My father's life was holding by a thread. He wanted to see me married. I don't know what I thought, when Marie told me she had waited for me.'

'I waited for you too, you promised you would write to me. We waited for you.'

'I know, I realised that I have made a mistake. A huge mistake. I have been very selfish and forgot to take care of you.'

Shanti stood still; her eyes lost in a faraway gaze. She could not think straight now, as she imbibed Sébastien's words. They rang like a discordant bell from a distance.

Veronique suddenly appeared on the doorstep, wiping her hands on her apron.

'Oh, here you are Shanti ... Sorry to interrupt, *Missier* Sébastien, I was looking for Shanti to come for her soup, she is still very weak. Do you mind if I take her in?'

'Not at all ... Shanti, I will see you tonight'

She took Shanti by the arm and led her inside the house. It ended the ex-lover's conversation. The baby started crying, and Veronique rushed to go and see him. Shanti walked to the kitchen and took her bowl of light chicken soup Veronique made her daily. It was a special type of broth made with black legged chicken, with dried jujube, goji berries, black mushrooms, ginger, carrots, potatoes and pumpkin cooked in wine. It was a Chinese recipe for women to recuperate after delivery. Instead of breakfast of baguette and butter, Veronique insisted she had that soup. Shanti sat at the kitchen table, looking at the fresh Bougainvillea flowers which were in the vase. Their fuchsia colours brought cheer to the room, and outside the sky had turned into a deep cerulean blue. It is going to be a hot bright sunny day. Shanti ate her soup slowly, meditating upon the words of Sebastien. 'Our child' he had said. Suddenly, Shanti felt that the soup had a pleasant taste. And she finished the bowl with a rekindled strength. The day was looking pleasant. Her heart felt lighter.

*

A woman's labour, her tea plucking, is located on one side of the international division of labour. She is variously a subaltern, working-class. She signals the margin. She is emblematic of a certain silence. Her stories sit in the shadows of impossible representations. Although Devika is today the mistress, she still does not gain so much popularity, being a woman. Land, sugar and tea estates are very gender biased. Club houses exist for men. They play, drink, smoke and converse among themselves. Women do not move among them as their equals. They are best seen as spouses enjoying a cup of tea, eating cake, and keeping their conversation mundane and domestic.

Restoring balance within the communities of tea workers also demand a male figure. It helps to disperse and cohere through work disciplines in factory and field, and shape village politics. All of which rests at the core of plantation patronage and its feudalism. With her new style of liberal thinking, Devika was risking losing a battle, if the workers did not respect her enough. She was firm in her ways of managing the estate. She was here to shake the old shackles of gender-based issues and prejudices at all levels.

The samples that she sent to the auctioneers through Sebastien fortunately, brought their rewards. She suddenly received orders that she had never dreamed could happen. All her new tea blends with local flavours were well accepted. There was definitely a great future for Bonne Espérance if everything went well. She would not need to take a bank loan as the payments for the orders arrived sooner than expected. It is with this news that Sebastien arrived, face flushed and burst running through the house looking for Devika.

He saw Shanti and Veronique and stopped on the spot.

'Where is Madame?'

'She has gone out.'

'We made it! We made it ….!'

'What have we made?' Asked Veronique while Shanti stood watching, impassable.

'I cannot tell you how happy I am Veronique. We have received orders from London, Nairobi and France. Bonne Espérance is saved! Please tell Madame Devika as soon as she comes.'

Sébastien left for the factory after gulping in a

full glass of chilled passion fruit juice drink that Veronique presented him on a tray. The news had lifted their spirits. That was tremendous news for all of their futures. Both women could not wait to tell Devika about the great news. Marcel knocked at the back door of the kitchen. Shanti went to open and saw the old man with a bunch of amaranth greens.

'Here, I got *brèdes-malbar* from the end of the vegetable garden. There are carrots too which are ready, if you want, I can pull them.' He said, wiping his sweaty forehead.

'Please come in Ton Marcel, have some fresh juice I have just made. The *brèdes-malbar* look very fresh, I shall cook them today. Thank you.'

Marcel came in, sat down and drank some chilled juice, Veronique offered him some biscuits too.

'No, thank you, I am controlling my sugar, the juice is enough. I don't want to end with unnecessary illness in my old age. You know my sweet tooth. How is the baby? I am with my work clothes, otherwise I would have held him a bit to say hello to Grand Père Marcel'

'Don't worry Ton, I will take him tomorrow morning for a small stroll down the garden, and you can see him. He is a good baby; he does not need too much fuss.'

'God bless, he shall grow into a strong boy to look after his mother, Shanti. You just watch how fast he will grow .... like a beanstalk.' Marcel was tactful not to ask whether the father had seen the baby. He left with some grilled peanuts Veronique gave him to snack on in between his breaks.

Sébastien became a father again within two months. Marie sent a telegram to announce the good news. He told Devika at dinner that Marie had a daughter, and that both mother and baby were doing well. He did not look very excited. That's what Veronique came to tell Shanti whispering, '*Missier* does not look so excited, I wonder why?' Shanti avoided the presence of Sébastien as much as she could. She stayed in the kitchen while Veronique was serving dinner.

'Congratulations! I believe you would be asking for leave to visit your wife and baby?' said Devika.

'No, not really. In fact, I have a lot of important work right now, we are going through the contracts of the new orders, I was to see them through myself. This is not the right time to take leave, we have waited so much for these orders.'

'Fair enough' Devika gave an appreciative nod and carried on eating. Dinner consisted of her favourite *étouffé* of *brèdes*, rice, dal with fried fish Veronique had cooked. A poor man's meal, as it's known. She was surprised by the look of detachment on Sébastien's face. Someone else would have been rushing to see his new born. But then, neither did her own husband do so, nor did Sebastien when baby Nishant was born. Maybe, he was being cautious, or it is that men process their feelings differently? Devika was sure that the young man would come talking about it all to her.

Indeed, Sébastien, taking a long tea under the veranda on the Sunday morning, felt the compulsion of confiding in Devika again. His initial infatuation of the early days when he arrived at the tea estate had given way to a brotherly affection for Devika. Things got clearer in his feelings when he met Shanti. Ever since then, he felt close to Devika and enjoyed her protective ways and wisdom.

Devika was finishing the hem of a saree, when Sébastien spoke 'Marie has given me an ultimatum. She wants me to choose between returning to her and the baby, or to stay here.' He looked at Devika, expecting her to reply. The latter lifted her eyes to receive this new development.

‘Oh really? So, what have you decided?’

‘I told her before we got married that I will never go back to cold, dull Brittany. That she will have to follow me if she wants to be with me. This remains unchanged. Besides, she doesn't like it here, we don’t have a future together living in Mauritius.’

‘That’s a bit rushed, don’t you think?’

‘I am never going to get a job I love so much, in Brittany. I like it here. Everything works for me. The freedom, the climate, the peacefulness, the motivation, the tea estate, the people, and you all’

‘But what about your family? Don’t you want to give it a thought again? Family comes before everything else. I am not sure you are thinking it through. You have a baby now. You have to be with your wife and child.’

‘You May find it hard to believe, but I have made a huge mistake and need atonement.

Marie is well looked after; she is educated and can go back to her teaching job. All her family and friends are around her. Here, she was miserable. We barely communicated before she left.'

'Think well before rushing into any decision you might regret afterwards.'

The tea estate had nothing to offer Marie besides Sébastien's company, and that would be limited to a few hours in the evening, unless something else came up to take even that away. There would be days when she would have to dine alone and go to bed long before he returned. Marie had been through it all before. She felt that she would go mad if she had too much time with nothing to do.

This distance had not done much to mend her relationship with Sébastien. It had always been more a marriage of convenience than love, and she had come to terms with this truth a long time ago.

Devika did not say any more words. It was very clear that the marriage was on the rocks.

That evening, Sébastien moved on to Shanti's bedroom. She was asleep. Beside her bed was a little cot with a white net over it. Inside it, also asleep, was the baby. The room was quiet except for the soft regular sound of Shanti's breathing. She looked pale, her forehead and upper lip were moist with perspiration; strands of hair clung wet against her neck. He sat down on the bed close to the cot. Gently he extended his little finger down into the cot and placed it against his son's tightly closed, dimpled fist. The tiny fingers unfurled and closed tightly on his finger. He felt his chest tighten with emotion. At that moment, he fell in love with his son.

Shanti stirred, woken up by the movement. "what are you doing here *Missier*?" she smiled, soon tears rolling down her cheeks.

He reached for a towel and began drying them.

He kissed her and stroked her head. Easing a pillow behind her back, he helped her to sit up. His ministrations were interrupted by a loud cry from the baby.

“He needs his feed. Pass him to me. Madame Devika told me that babies are hungry all the time. Certainly, this is one hungry baby. I fed her less than three hours ago.”

Handing the baby over, he said, dipping a hand into his pocket, he drew out a small red packet. Inside was a little gold anklet with a tiny bell. He said, “this is for the baby so you can always hear him.”

It was quiet in the house, so quiet that the sucking of the baby could be heard. Shanti put down the empty bottle, wiped Nishant’s lips and patted his back until he burped.

‘Thank you *Missier* Sébastien, am sure Nishant would love his anklet very much.’ The sleeping baby looked like a little angel. Wet lashes lay like fans on his pink cheeks. Before leaving,

Sébastien leaned over and kissed him on his forehead. Until now, Shanti had steadfastly avoided having close contact with Sébastien. She was afraid that she might reveal her feelings. It was fate, she reasoned, that father and son should be reconciled.

31 REDEMPTION

Shanti and Sébastien grew more comfortable with each other's presence. The young man took to visiting baby Nishant twice each day. Morning, before he had breakfast, and in the evening when he came back from work. He started spending more time playing with the baby, to the secret joy of Shanti.

'Shanti, can you ever forgive me?' He said one evening, holding Nishant in his arms. The two looked like a picture-perfect father and son.

'*Missier*, I forgave you a long time ago. *Bhagwan* wanted this to happen to me. Maybe, that was destiny. I would like Nishant to know you as his father, so that the world doesn't spit on him for being an illegitimate child.' He put his arms around her shoulders and kissed the top of her head. "I promise I will look after you and Nishant."

Shanti spent her time looking after her own baby as well as Beti who had started walking now. She also helped around the house, when the young ones were asleep. Devika felt like peace had come back to the household. A quiet routine installed itself with cheer and playfulness around baby and toddler.

Sébastien and Shanti got together, as soon as he had told her that his marriage with Marie was over. That she would not come back, and their divorce procedure was completed. Shanti felt sad but there was little she could do. The bond between them became stronger than it had ever been. Shanti thought that it was even better than their early time together, because now there was a deeper understanding brought on by shared misfortune and a son together. She also sensed some sort of desperation that made them cling to each other.

'Sébastien' Shanti said slowly, feeding the baby, 'I think that you should go and see your daughter. She needs you. Go back to your family. I feel guilty to have taken the place of Marie.'

Sébastien got up from the bed. He drew a dressing gown over his pyjamas to keep out the cool morning breeze. He went up to the window and drew the thick curtains apart and said:

'Look at this house, its garden, and these wide-open spaces that have become a part of me. Look at the mountains and the forest. Bonne Espérance is my garden of Eden. There is no perfume better than the fragrance of the waxy, white flowers of the tea bush. What can replace the aroma that rises from freshly brewed, ruby-amber tea? I love the sensation when I crumble our brown, black and green teas between my fingers. How can I live so far away from these plants, without seeing the seedlings planted, bushes pruned, and the crates clearly marked before they are loaded onto trucks and sent on their way? This place is my haven, Shanti. Think of all this before you tell me to leave this place and this kind of life forever.'

When Sebastien stressed the word 'this' in his last sentence, Shanti knew that he was referring to their relationship as well. Shanti never mentioned Marie again.

It broke Sébastien's heart that he would never really know his daughter, and he would only have himself to blame for the distance that would grow over the years.

A month later, Sébastien drove the jeep to a small church to christen Nishant. Shanti knew the meaning of the ceremony. She resisted conversion for herself but agreed that the child needed to have a religion of some sort. Her son had to belong somewhere. Sébastien had told her to wear something off white, sober for the ceremony. They met with Marcel, Bhai Hamid, Veronique, Devika and her daughter, Paul and his wife, at the church. All dressed up smartly for the occasion. Shanti's heart swelled with joy. After the baptism, the priest called Shanti and Sébastien to the altar, and Veronique quickly took out a fresh flower posy and handed it to Shanti. The young woman took it thinking it was part of the ceremony. Only to realise later what the priest was reading next, were vows of marriage. Sébastien pulled out a golden band from his pocket, while Devika guided her daughter with a small cushion where a gold band rested.

Shanti could not contain her surprise, beaming with happiness, blushing profusely. They were married without any pretence, with only their well-wishers present to bless them.

After christening, Devika took the new parents and newlyweds to a small Chinese restaurant in the neighbouring town. She presented Shanti with a cream saree embroidered with red flowers in sequins. Nishant, now called Élouan Laval meaning light in Breton, received a silver bowl and spoon from his father. Shanti was touched by Sébastien's display of affection. He had a gift for her as well. It was a pair of gold earrings.

'I've never given you any jewellery before,' he said sheepishly. 'I thought that you would like this design. Thank you, Veronique, for helping me choose them.'

Shanti had never eaten in a restaurant before and hoped that she would not make any mistakes. The men did not notice her squirming as they laughed and talked amiably. It was a simple outing for them but a rather daunting experience for her. The baby lay on the padded bench between Sebastien and her. Her world had just changed, and she was feeling elated by the events. Furthermore, she knew that although she has been away from the community since she fell pregnant, people probably knew about her affair. No one could escape gossip within such a small village.

Sébastien, making his relationship with her official today, was a sort of cleansing of its illegitimacy. People would change their attitude towards Shanti after her marriage with Sebastien, that she knew for sure, and felt relieved about it.

Mawsi called in at the villa to visit, bringing some gifts. Shanti had sent a message through Bhai Hamid. *Mawsi* said she was not worried about rumour mongers anymore. She could walk down the village with her head held high. Peace had come back in Shanti's life. Sebastien was a loving father, and the child became very attached to him. It only seemed natural that another baby should arrive soon. A daughter was born. Shanti decided to name the baby Devi, after the woman who had helped her so much. Veronique was asked to be the godmother, once again.

Bonne Espérance gave hope to everyone whose

lives were tied to it. Nobody would despise Shanti anymore to have been a white man's mistress. Erasing the scar of her own birth. Devika believed in the good luck that the tea estate brought to her. And truly so, to others.

A real paradise laid at their feet to enjoy for the rest of their lives.

ABOUT TEA

Mauritius has stood with a resilient face after gaining independence, carving itself a place in the sun, breaking free from its colonial past. It rested its strength on the sugar crop of the French settlers. While it managed to shine itself towards a prosperous land from sugar cane, it also has come along with one of the best teas in the world. Due to its size, the island never claimed its due place in the gold reserves of tea connoisseurs.

After water, tea is humankind's most consumed drink, making the tea tree one of the world's most important cultivated plants. There are strong parallels between tea and wine. Both are taken for pleasure. At the higher levels of connoisseurship, the nuances of flavour, aroma and texture of both come under intense scrutiny. The wine concept of terroir – the soil, climate and other local conditions that give each wine its character – applies every bit as much to tea, in which connoisseurs enjoy reaching back through the cup to the land where the leaf grew. This is one of the most beautiful ideas in tea drinking, that the careful picking and processing create leaves that awaken in hot water, and they then release their original natural world to you, the tea drinker. That is, the nature that surrounds the plant, from soil to air to the terroir. The finest teas are tended by artisan growers in small plots with no fertilizers, and the terroirs.

The taste and experience of pure nature, with all its exquisite flavours and aromas, are at the heart of the enjoyment of tea.

There was a time when maps of the world were redrawn in the name of plants, when two empires, Britain and China, went to war over two flowers: the poppy and the camellia. The poppy, Papaver somniferum, was processed into opium, a narcotic used widely throughout the Orient in the eighteenth and nineteenth centuries. The drug was grown and manufactured in India, a subcontinent of princely states united under the banner of Greater Britain, in 1757. Opium was marketed, solely and exclusively, under the aegis of England's Empire in India by the Honourable East India Company. The camellia, Camellia sinensis, is also known as tea. The Empire of China had a near complete monopoly on tea, as it was the only country to grow, pick, process, cook, and in all other ways manufacture, wholesale and export 'the liquid jade'. For nearly two hundred years, the East India Company sold opium to China and bought tea with the proceeds. China, in turn, bought opium from British traders out of India and paid for the drug with the silver profits from tea.

Although the history of tea is as great as the summation of all of the tea consumed, the story of tea, as it is most often told, invariably begins with one of a handful of genesis myths. These myths are good stories but, more important, they provide significant insight into the cultural importance of tea throughout the world.

Today tea is grown in forty-five countries around the world and is the second most commonly drunk beverage after water. It's a $90 billion global market. Until just a few years ago, India was the world's largest producer of tea. Although overtaken by China, it still produces about a billion kilograms—more than two billion pounds—a year. Tea can generally be classified in six distinct types: black, oolong, green, yellow, white, and pu-erh. All come from the same plant. The difference lies in processing. Nearly all of India's tea is black tea, which means that the leaves have been withered and fermented and certain characteristic flavours allowed to develop. (Green tea is neither withered nor fermented, and oolong is only semi *fermented.) Yet the wide geographic and climatic range of India's tea-growing areas, from lowland forest to Himalayan foothills, means that it produces a variety of distinctive black teas.*

More than 90 percent of the world's (and the majority of India's) black teas are produced by a method called CTC (cut, tear, curl). In the mid-twentieth century, with the growing popularity of tea bags, a new way to process leaves was developed that made it more convenient for filling the small sachets as well as brewing a quicker, stronger infused liquid. Instead of rolling and twisting the leaves, a machine chops and cuts them into small pieces with blades revolving at different speeds. The result is chocolate-brown granules of tea, even and pebbly rather than wiry and twisted like orthodox leaves. Tea is more than merely a drink it's a soother and an energizer, a marker of time present at the most quotidian moments of daily life and at the most special.

GENESIS OF TEA

Confucian: One of the more popular of these myths, and the first story I heard told about tea, starts with the Chinese inventor of farming and medicine, Shennong, sitting in the shade of a Camellia Sinensis tree. While Shennong sat under the tree, a leaf allegedly fell into his cup of boiled water and began to steep. Being a man of medicine, Shennong noted that the leaf not only created a beautiful green colour, but that it made him feel refreshed, stimulated, and full of vigour. Thus, tea was born.

This Chinese myth is important not because it describes the origins of tea, but because it helps link the present to the mythical past and reminds us of the power and security of ancestry.

This fable guides us into seeing the world

through a Confucian lens and provides a glimpse into the Chinese worldview and their reverence toward tea.

Buddhist: Another genesis myth that has repeatedly been shared with me provides that the founder of Buddhism, Siddhartha Gautama, sat down after a long meditative walk through the mountains and unwillingly fell asleep. When he awoke, he felt furious at his lack of control and discipline, and at his weakness. So, in a fit of rage he ripped out his eyelashes and threw them into the wind. From these eyelashes grew the first tea plants. Like the aforementioned Confucian fable, this myth provides a glimpse into a particular worldview. Generally, the myth illustrates the fundamental Buddhist belief that one cannot find true enlightenment until one has escaped the bonds of the material world—an idea represented by the Buddha's removal of his eyelashes. Interestingly, it has been stated that tea's ability to provide energy and focus made it the perfect accompaniment to the intellectually rigorous demands of Buddhism and is what helped Buddhism spread from south Asia through all of Asia. Similar to the Confucian myth, this myth is not just a story about the origins of tea; it is a lesson that guides us into understanding the Buddhist worldview and their reverence toward tea.

Most books about the history of tea in Europe begin sometime around 1600 when England created the East India Company, an organization with authority to acquire territory, coin money, maintain armies and forts, form foreign alliances, and declare war. Through these powers the East India Company started trading silver for tea in the late 1600s and began to acquire large wealth for the English Crown. The East India Company was so successful trading tea, however, that by the middle of the 1800s England's silver reserves were virtually depleted. To fix this imbalance, the East India

Company tapped into its resources from land it acquired in Bengal—namely large fields of poppy plants, the seeds of which could be used for processing opium—and began trading opium for tea, a practice that resulted in severe opium addiction throughout China in the 1800s, the two famous Opium Wars (1839–1842 and 1856–1860), and, eventually, the cessation of Chinese foreign trade.

The irony that the English sought to acquire tea by enabling opium addiction throughout China seems to be lost in most discussions about tea in the Western world, but it is fundamental in understanding current tea trends. It is generally agreed that the Opium Wars were the precursor to the demise of Imperial China; that the vacuum left from this political instability eventually led to the Chinese Communist Revolution; that the Communist Revolution led to China's Cultural Revolution in the 1960s; and that these revolutions almost completely destroyed

China's specialty "bourgeois" tea industry. With trade between China and the West stopped, generations of people in the Western world could no longer experience China's famous teas. Only after the Chinese began liberalizing its trade restrictions in the 1980s and 1990s did the Chinese tea industry begin to recover and did the Western world again begin to discover the joys of these teas. Thus, in the past fifteen to twenty years the world is again beginning to "discover" the great Chinese teas.

Prior to using opium to extract tea from China, the British governor general of India began investigating whether it was possible to break China's tea monopoly by growing tea in India. In anticipation of this experiment, he annexed what is present-day Assam (1824) and purchased a deed from the raja of Sikkim for land around the present-day region of Darjeeling in the state of West Bengal (1835).

*

Tea became chic with Charles II's marriage to the Portuguese princess and tea addict Catherine of Braganza in 1662. Along with the ports of Bombay and Tangier and the free right to trade in Brazil and the East Indies, her dowry included a chest of tea. The drink was new to the country, and so, too, to the English language. According to the Oxford English Dictionary, the first use of the word tea—or rather, it's early variant, chaa—dates back to the 1598 translation of Jan Huyghen van Linschoten's Discourse of Voyages into East & West Indies, which referred to the drink as being "made with the powder of a certain hearbe called Chaa." The spelling quickly ran through various forms—tay, tey, té, thé, the, teee, thea—before finally landing on its more familiar form, tea. Much of Western Europe derived their word from the term for tea in Amoy (now Xiamen) following the Dutch (thee), who traded it to them from their early base in Bantam, Java: thee (German), te (Danish and Swedish), té (Spanish), tè

(Italian), and thé (French). The Hindi and Bengali terms for tea (chai and cha, respectively) derive from the second source for the word, the Cantonese ch'a (pronounced chah). So does Japanese (cha), Arabic (shai or chai), Persian (chay), and Russian (chai). Portugal (chá) is a Western European exception, but then they first obtained tea from Canton (today called Guangzhou). The modern English pronunciation of tea took longer to catch up. When coffeehouse habitué Alexander Pope wrote The Rape of the Lock in 1714, he rhymed tea with away and obey. Fifty years later, the vowel had tightened, and the rake, rebel, and poet Charles Churchill wrote this sprightly couplet about reading tea leaves:

"Matrons, who toss the cup, and see

The grounds of fate in grounds of tea."

By the time Churchill penned his verse, the price of tea had dropped from the dearly unaffordable to the merely expensive, and soon the drink moved from being a luxury of the aristocracy and upper class to a necessity of the working class. The British were enjoying a two- (or three- four) cups-a-day habit. Certainly, one habit set the British apart from Chinese and Japanese tea drinkers: they were adding milk. Was it to avoid staining their fine bone-china cups? To soften tea's astringency. Help digestion? No one would ever know. Preparing tea had its own rituals, but they were never permeated with religious or philosophical elements as in China and Japan. Yet in Britain tea gained a relevance unsurpassed in the rest of Europe, and the British drew as much pleasure and even dependence from the drink as those in any place in Asia. As much as they pursued sugar, tea became the next addiction of the higher class. Cones of sugar were displayed in lavish tables of nobles and aristocrats. Catherine of Braganza's use of tea as a court beverage, rather than a medicinal drink, influenced its popularity in literary circles around 1685. Whenever it was consumed in the court, it was "conspicuously on display" so as to show it off. Wealthy ladies' desire to show off their luxurious commodities in front of other ladies also increased demand for tea and made it more popular. Another factor that made tea desirable among the elite crowd was the addition of sugar, another luxurious commodity which was already well-established among the upper classes.

Accordingly, tea drinking became a central aspect of aristocratic society in England by the 1680s, particularly among women who drank it while gossiping in the home. Though by the beginning of the 18th century tea was already gaining popularity on its own, the addition of sugar helped tea's popularity to soar. The English began adding sugar to their tea between 1685 and the early 18th century. At this time, sugar was already being used to enhance the flavour of other foods among the elite and had a reputation as an ostentatious luxury. Because both tea and sugar had status implications it made sense to drink them together, and the growth in the import of tea parallels that of sugar in the 18th century, which itself was booming due to the growth of sugar plantations in the Americas.

Perhaps spaces of aristocratic consumption were created into cultivated domains of social refinement because they refracted the ostensibly pristine conditions of labour in one site of production. These were idealized cosmologies of labour, immaculate myths, if you will, which underscored the romance of feminized work and permeated the rarefied domains of aristocratic tea consumption. The 'at home' teas of leisured Victorian and Edwardian households were afternoon parties with varying degrees of formality. They featured thin bread and butter (the slices rolled, so as not to soil the kid gloves all ladies wore), little sandwiches, toast cut into fingers, and small cakes. Some houses offered heartier food, such as scones fresh from the oven, and bread to be cut and made into more substantial sandwiches, more appealing to masculine taste. These teas are the inspiration for many now offered in smart cafés and hotels throughout Britain, featuring delicate finger food: tiny sandwiches, pastries, fragile little cakes and biscuits, maybe with scones, or pieces cut from larger cakes, dainty and pretty, as if to say, this is not really a meal. The history of afternoon tea is obscure; although a few morsels of light food were offered with a drink of tea in the eighteenth century, it is often dated to about 1840, when Anna Russell, Duchess of Bedford, found she suffered a 'sinking feeling' in the long, food-free hours between breakfast and dinner. The latter had become an evening meal in fashionable life (lunch as it is now understood did not exist). Anna's solution to the problem was an afternoon drink of tea, accompanied by a little food. While visiting the Duke of

Rutland at Belvoir Castle in Leicestershire, she invited her female friends to partake, and so originated afternoon tea, or 'five o'clock tea', as it is sometimes known. Tea gardens flourished at this time, their pleasant surroundings providing musical and other entertainments. Food, especially bread and butter, was offered alongside tea, but seems to have been secondary. The tax on tea was massively reduced in 1784 and tea drinking was taken up by all classes. The price of tea dropped again when the British established plantations in India and Ceylon (now Sri Lanka) in the mid-nineteenth century. Deep coloured, richly flavoured black teas taken with milk and sugar became the accustomed drink for many.

During the Song era, numerous tea plantations were cultivated on Mount Meng and "the heavy mists blanketing the peak were believed to conjure the Immortals so as to protect the tea trees from marauding strangers." Another tea, a semi fermented (oolong) tea from Fukien's Mount Wu-I, is called T'ieh-Kuan-Yin (Iron Goddess of Mercy), because it is grown near the temple of the goddess Kuan Yin. The story, passed into legend, is as follows: A disciple of the goddess cared for a ramshackle and ruined temple. The goddess, pleased at his devotion, appeared to him in a dream, telling him of a treasure he would find in a nearby cave that he should share with everyone.

Discovering a small tea sapling, the disappointed devotee nevertheless tended it to its fullness and thereupon discovered its golden aroma. Soon, he had a thriving business in tea. If tea fed the "dignity of government," it was the elegant rites of aristocrats and scholars that threaded the cultural economies of its consumption.

Private teahouses of the wealthy were surrounded by gardens with lotus ponds, grottoes, bamboo groves, and miniature trees.

Nature, thus transformed to an exquisite art, would be the perfect site for the imbibing of tea.

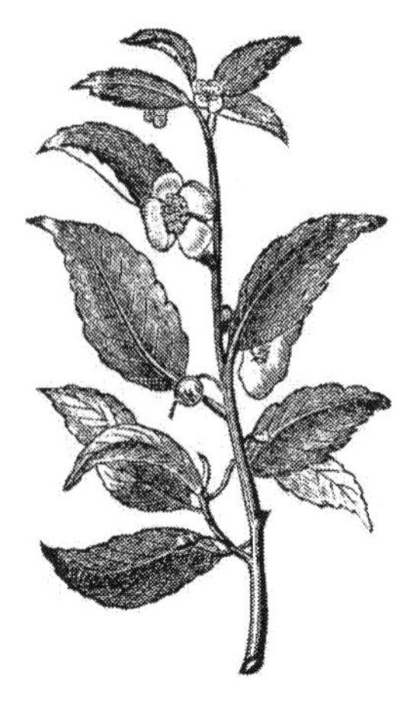

The Tea Plant

To fully understand how the Camellia sinensis plant developed from a medicinal herb to become the most widely consumed beverage, after water, around the world, we need to examine the plant itself in more depth. The qualities of tea as a drink can be broadly attributed to three main factors: the variety of tea plant, its growing conditions and how it is processed, and we will explore these here.

VARIETY AND CULTIVAR

Camellia refers to the genus of the plant and sinensis details the species. This can be further broken down into varieties or cultivars. Varieties are the differences among the same species that are found naturally in the world;

if they are propagated (bred deliberately) by the grower, they become cultivated varieties, or cultivars. This happens when a grower notices desirable variation in a plant (such as yield, or frost, insect or disease resistance) and chooses to preserve them through cultivation. This is done by using cuttings rather than seeds from the plants. Cuttings create identical clones of the mother plant, whereas seedlings do not always pass on their parents' desirable characteristics. This is because tea is a cross-pollinated plant.

The two main varieties used in the making of tea are Camellia sinensis var. sinensis and Camellia sinensis var. assamica. Sinensis means 'from China', and assamica is derived from Assam, the northern India state, reflecting the origins of each variety. Cultivars are created from these varieties. Take, for example, the Taiwanese Shanlinxi oolong. This can be accurately described as Camellia sinensis var. sinensis Qing Xin. The genus is

Camellia, the species is sinensis, the variety is sinensis, and the cultivar is Qing Xin. Camellia sinensis var. sinensis tends to have relatively small, light and narrow leaves and is thought to be native to western Yunnan, China. It has a greater resistance to cold and drought than other varieties, so outside China it is grown widely in Taiwan and Japan. A notable area of use is Darjeeling, India. When left to grow it reaches a maximum height of 6 metres. The characteristics of its leaf mean that it is mainly used to produce green and white tea. Camellia sinensis var. assamica has much larger leaves that tend to be thicker. This is the variety that was first recorded as growing in Assam by the Scotsman Robert Bruce. It can grow into a tree of around 30 metres tall and thrives in more moist, warmer and tropical regions like its native Assam, and also Sri Lanka and Africa. It is most suited to making black teas.

CLIMATE

To thrive, a tea plant needs at least 5 hours of sun per day at an average temperature of around 18–20°C. Also preferable is plenty of rain (150–250 centimetres per year), a relative humidity of 70–90 percent and a dry season that is no longer than three months. This means that tropical or subtropical regions are best. Variations in climate that are not too extreme develop flavour. The stresses caused by a drop or rise in temperature, or a period without rain, stimulate a reaction from the plant in order to retain chlorophyll, changing the flavour produced.

ALTITUDE

Many of the plantations producing the best tea are found at higher altitudes. The conditions here often slow the growth of tea plants, leading to a higher concentration of the aromatic oils and beneficial, flavoursome nutrients found in the leaves. High-altitude teas such as those from Darjeeling (600–2,000 metres) and Assam (1,000–2,300 metres), are considered among the best in the world for flavour complexity in flavour and taste.

PROCESSING

Processing is an important way of classifying teas, according to the level of oxidation (when the plucked leaves are exposed to the atmosphere for minutes or hours, withering and discolouring from green to black).

White teas are the least processed, produced from the shoots and top few leaves of the plant, which are simply dried.

They are generally, but not invariably, low in caffeine and produce a drink that is pale in colour with a delicate taste and aroma.

Green teas are now considered a healthy choice in the range of teas, as processing – which involves a stage of heating to halt oxidation – inhibits the development of caffeine and preserves antioxidants, as well as the green colour.

Matcha is a type of Japanese green tea, in which the leaves are ground, and the powder mixed with water.

Oolong teas are partially oxidised and have more complex flavours than green teas; the best are beautifully fragrant. The leaves can be re-infused several times.

Black teas are by far the most commonly consumed teas in the UK. These are fully oxidised, giving a higher caffeine content and a range of coppery and chestnut brown colours and malty flavours familiar to British tea drinkers.

Tea is also graded according to leaf size, shape and the part of the plant it comes from, from whole leaf to dust; despite its unpromising name the latter can be sought after to produce dark, strong tea ideal for drinking with milk. It is also used in tea bags.

Larger leaves are sometimes rolled into balls to give pearl teas or Gunpowder tea; the process aids flavour retention and makes for easier packing.

Flower teas consist of hand-rolled and tied leaves, green or white, which unfurl in water to give a bloom-like effect.

Orange Pekoe, despite its colloquial use as a name for various black teas, actually is a description of the grade of leaf rather than a blend.

Some areas produce single-estate teas; these are unblended and vary from year to year.

Blended teas are produced by mixing two or more tea varieties and include several British favourites.

English Breakfast Tea is a blended black tea intended to be drunk with milk, a good accompaniment to sweet foods.

Earl Grey is a mild-tasting black tea scented

with bergamot oil, giving a citrus note.

Lapsang Soochong has a distinctive pungent, smoky taste created by drying black tea leaves over pine-wood fires.

Russian Caravan, another pungent black tea with a slightly smoky flavour and dark colour, originated from the tradition of carrying tea overland from China to Russia. They are brewed and taken with milk. Or with a touch of Vodka.

Jasmine tea, typically a white or green tea, is scented by contact with fresh jasmine blossoms, which only release their fragrance at night.

Other drinks produced by steeping dried leaves or plant matter in hot water are technically known as infusions. One which has recently become popular in Britain is Rooibos, or Red Bush (Aspalathus linearis), of South African origin.

The leaves are plucked, oxidised and dried to give a drink that is high in antioxidants and caffeine-free.

How to make a good pot of tea

Making a pot of tea is a comforting ritual embedded deep in British culture, and everyone knows how to do this – or do they? This is not about a tea bag in a mug of hot water (however quick and convenient this may be). Really good tea deserves attention and thought. The general instructions for making tea in the British way have remained more or less consistent since the mid-nineteenth century and refer specifically to black teas such as Assam. Once you are equipped with a suitably sized teapot, this is how to go about it. The water should be freshly drawn. Soft water is best. Those who are really serious about tea use filtered tap

water or spring water. Fill the kettle and bring it to the boil. The tea should be made as soon as the water boils (if it is allowed to go on boiling, or re-boiled, the tea will taste flat), so the pot must be ready. Warm it, either by filling it with hot water and leaving it to stand for a few minutes before pouring the water away, or by swilling hot water round the pot and emptying it. Take the pot to the kettle.

Add the tea: the usual instruction is to add one teaspoonful of loose-leaf tea per person and one for the pot (omit the latter if not keen on very strong tea).

Pour in the freshly boiled water from the kettle and leave to stand for 3–5 minutes if drinking it black, a minute or two longer if adding milk. Then pour through a strainer into cups. Sugar and thin lemon slices for black tea, or sugar and milk otherwise. Tea which has been left to stand for a long develops a bitter flavour.

Printed in Great Britain
by Amazon

59101625R00239